Brendan's life is about to change. After dealing with traumatic experiences throughout his adolescent years, Brendan sees his friend, Aliyah, in a different light. Hoping for his luck to change and searching for ultimate happiness, Brendan and Aliyah embark on a journey together, but will it be everything he's been searching for?

Warning: this book contains suicide.

Privileged
Copyright © 2019 Mathew Di-Giusto
ISBN: 978-1-4874-2389-6
Cover art by Martine Jardin

Published by eXtasy Books Inc or
Devine Destinies, an imprint of eXtasy Books Inc

Look for us online at:
www.eXtasybooks.com or www.devinedestinies.com

PRIVILEGED

BY

MATHEW DI-GIUSTO

CHAPTER ONE: THE BEGINNING

Dear friend?
I wanted to thank you for listening. Many people don't realize this, but it's a virtue all too often taken for granted. Although we will never meet, I hope you realise you already mean more to me than ninety-nine percent of the people I have ever met. I feel we are eternally connected, for you get to hear my last words. I just need you to understand something you will never understand. For as I write this, I still don't, and I never will.

I will never forget the first time I felt helpless. It was a beautiful day without a cloud in the sky, and I had been at school all day. I went to a nice school located right in the center of our city. Our city, of approximately sixty thousand people, had a dozen primary and secondary schools. It was the second biggest city in the state.

I used to ride my bike to school with two of my friends, and we decided to stop at the park on the way home to play some football. We grabbed some treats from the local shop and kicked the footy around until seven o'clock, time to head home because of our curfews. I was all of nine, and Mum never let me stay out after dark. There was always a rule in our household. No matter what, we sat down at the dinner table and ate as a family.

Mum was the absolute epitome of what a mother should be. She had a good job and was always home by five to make sure dinner was on the table by seven. She cooked,

1

cleaned, and drove us to all our sports. I did seven, to be exact. Never for a moment did I question how much she adored and cherished us kids. We always tried to take care of the chores to give Mum and Dad some time to relax after long days.

Tuesday nights were different. Mum and Dad were the treasurer and secretary of our football club. They had to step out to a committee meeting. This happened frequently, and I was left in the care of my older brother and sister. Ben was thirteen and had just started secondary school. He got into the best one in the region, and Mum and Dad could not have been any prouder.

Puberty hit Ben in the summer, and didn't he love it? He went from being this chubby kid whose hair looked like it had a fight with a lawnmower, to the jock of the school with exceptional muscle tone for a thirteen-year-old.

My sister, Theresea, was eleven. She was short with brunette hair and one of the best netball players and swimmers in state.

After dark, you'd never see me out of the lounge room. I slept there as we didn't have enough bedrooms. I loved it. It was a massive room, and the computer was there. When I could no longer run around outside, I owned the computer. My favourite game was a mythological war one, and I'll never forget the irony of the level I was playing when Ben came in that evening.

There's this level where you're supposed to avenge this hero and his closest kinsmen because as the level starts, they're slaughtered. No matter what you do, you can never save them. It was impossible. I was about halfway through avenging them when my brother ripped me off the computer chair and threw me onto my bed. He covered me in pillows before throwing punch after punch.

Some people might argue that it was a nice thing to do by

putting the pillows down, but trust me when I say they did not soften the blows, not one bit. My sister bolted in halfway during my screaming and tried to pull Ben off, but he lashed out at her. As he pushed her, she fell back and hit the corner of the computer desk, splitting her head open.

Ben never paused. He immediately went back to throwing punches at me. The most upsetting part was seeing my sister cry. It broke my heart. He told us that if we told Mum and Dad, he'd do it again the next time they were out. The saddest part was, it was the truth. We had to lie to save our ass from another beating. Theresea and I patched up our wounds in the bathroom, and when Mum and Dad got home, we had told them we fell out of the tree and hit a few of the rocks in the garden. They were upset at us for playing outside after dark.

These beatings continued. I tried telling Mum and Dad at some stage, but they couldn't keep eyes on me every hour of the day. I guess you could say with beating after beating, I got used to them, but one day my brother went too far. We lived in the suburbs, which made it lucky for me. I was outside racing my scooter around the pool when Ben came home from his girlfriend's house. I knew something was up, and I always knew when I was in harm's way.

You see, later in life when Ben was diagnosed with intermittent explosive disorder, it all became a bit clearer. One of the ticks for when he feels the attention is not on him is to take it out on whomever the attention is on. Apparently, I was my parent's favorite, and I never heard the end of it.

When he was upset, he bit his bottom lip, and you could see it in his eyes. It makes me sick to my stomach still thinking about his grey eyes and seeing nothing but anger. He chased me around the pool for what felt like a lifetime before he finally caught and tackled me. He dragged me over to the pool, laid me down beside it, and started pushing my head underwater. I don't recall too much of the incident other than the breaks in between him forcing my head underwater. They got shorter and shorter. I was screaming loudly hoping to get the attention of my neighbors, hoping to get the attention of a savior. Luckily for me, my prayers were answered.

A man named Kevin popped his head over the fence and told Ben if he didn't stop, he'd come over there and show him how tough he really was. Kevin stayed with me for twenty minutes until my parents arrived home. I was hysterical, an absolute mess, and it was agreed that Theresea and I were to not be left alone in the house. We had to go to Nan and Pop's after school from then on. Although it was a major inconvenience on everybody at times, I always enjoyed heading to Nan and Pop's. It could have been where my mother learned it, or to be so caring could be the duty of every grandparent in the world, but they had one agenda, to spoil Theresea and me.

CHAPTER TWO: THREE THOUSAND, FOUR HUNDRED AND EIGHTY-TWO KILOMETERS.

I was eleven when my parents came and dropped a bombshell on us.

"I've been offered a position in Victoria. It's a really exciting opportunity, but we need to know you kids are okay with it before I take the role."

Dad explained this in a very calm manner as if the job had been on offer for months and he had practiced his speech every night since. The rest of the conversation that night went on for hours, and we were given a week to decide. Many factors affected our decision to move, one of them being that my brother had been expelled almost a week before. Mum and Dad thought it was appropriate to get him out of his environment. After a long week, we decided to pack up and move across the country. Three thousand four hundred and eighty-two kilometers, to be exact. We went from a three-bedroom one-bathroom house, to a seven-bedroom four-bathroom house. It also had a study, a theatre room, and a pool, all made possible by Dad's new job. They paid for a lot of it.

Our first few days in Victoria were hectic. We went straight from the airport to our grandma's house where we were met my dad's side of the family. They were a big family. Grandma was one of eleven kids, and trust me when I say each one of those siblings went on to have quite large families, too. Not to mention their kids followed suit. Almost everyone was a new face to me. No one ever made the journey to Western Australia. It was too far away. Crossing the Nullarbor Plain was a pain, as it was seventeen-hundred-kilometers of just desert. Not a tree, just a few shrubs and very rarely a roadhouse. Western Australia. You could take a plane to New Zealand in half the time it takes to fly to Perth.

The rest of those first days were then taken up by shopping. We bought a new couch, a microwave, cooking utensils, beds—pretty much anything you can think of got an upgrade. At the end of the week came our present to help us adjust to our new lives. Ben got a promise of flights every school holiday's back to Western Australia to be with his girlfriend. Theresea got a laptop and an upgraded phone plan to keep in contact with all her besties. As for me, I chose one of the best computers around, along with a comfy desk and chair.

I continued with my love for gaming by purchasing a new game and locking myself away in my room all summer, only seeing the light of day at the start of February for school. I struggled to recognize myself when I emerged from that room. In two months, I came out a chubby teenager twenty kilograms heavier with long, uncut, scruffy hair and a bad case of facial acne. After being in isolation for so long, I didn't even know how to hold a conversation anymore.

The first day of school was the easiest. I had hoped just to fit in like I did at my old school. I didn't realize that confident, sporty kid had gone into hiding. I went to school thinking how easy it would be to make friends and enjoy my schooling. Jesus Christ, have I ever been so wrong? All the friendship groups were already decided. They'd either gone to primary school together, met at orientation, or connected on the bus ride there.

I rode to school, locked up my bike, and walked into school with my head down. There were large groups of guys and girls, all talking having a good time, some even playing some down ball on the courts. Everyone seemed to know each other. As for me, not one person. I sat up the back of my homeroom in the corner with my head fixed in my book. As homeroom began, my teacher, Mr. Jones, called on me to stand up.

"Everyone quiet, please. Although all of you are new to our college, many of us met on orientation day. Well, one student, however, didn't get that chance, and he stands before me now. Brendan has traveled a long way from Western Australia, and I want you all to make him feel welcome. You may take your seat now, Brendan."

Could you ever just smack someone in the face? I've always been a docile kid. I never got in anyone's way and kept to myself, but as Mr. Jones continued, Tom, the college hottie, leant back in his chair and whispered, "Oi, Brendan, maybe you could have run here. Might've helped."

I never said a word, just sat quietly and listened to the people within earshot snicker at the cheap shot at my weight. I certainly wasn't prepared for what high school had planned for me. Days went by, even weeks, but high school just got harder. At the start, I was optimistic about the possibilities of having friends and forgetting about Western Australia. Instead, my lunchtimes were spent hiding away in the library so they couldn't find me. I would always run to my bike to get out of that hell and back home to my serenity as soon as possible.

I was seven weeks into my first year of high school. I remember clearly because my parents gave my dad's old phone to me for my birthday. My first mobile phone, it was six months old and a brilliant little thing. A new present never leaves a teenager's side for days, and my phone was not going to be an exception. Tom caught me using it between third and fourth period. That was a bad mistake. He and his little rat pack followed me into the library and cornered me before taking my phone. They laughed as one of them threw it to the next guy. Although I was big, I was a year younger and gave up a good half a head to these guys. James, Josh, Mitch, and Tom were very big boys and didn't even care.

The words are still clear as day in my mind. "Fuck back off to where you came from," and "You could catch this, Brendan, if it was a cake."

One of the library ladies came to my rescue but arguably a few minutes too late. My pride and dignity were tarnished. I wanted to leave and never return. I still had two more periods which I begrudgingly moped to.

I just had to keep asking myself, why am I here? Why do I deserve this? High school isn't for me. Just grab your bike and ride home. It's hard to explain, but our school is on a hill. The seventh-year building is right next to the path I ride home. However, I lock my bike up near the twelfth year building down the other end of the school. Normally, I would stroll through the school, unlock my bike, and begin to cycle home. Not that day. I sprinted as fast as I could, choking back tears. I needed to be by myself for a while. It took me eleven minutes to get home at full pace, but that day I wanted it done in under ten. I began my ride down the hill. I was suddenly hit in the stomach at full speed with a solid tree branch. It was the rat pack. I fell over the handlebars, off my bike, and I couldn't move. I was in shock and too much pain.

The bike was on top of me, and there was nothing left of my helmet. My backpack had broken open, and my books were everywhere. My arm felt like it was broken, and there was blood flowing from both my arms and my head. I was unable to see properly due to the sun shining directly in my eyes, but I recognized the voice. I felt a swift kick to the ribs before I heard, "You don't want to be the guy who tells on us and gets us another detention. Watch your back."

Nothing else was said and nothing else was done. I was just left to lie there in pain for what felt like forever. Eventually, a few more people followed the same route and found me. They rushed to my side, removed the bike off me, and helped me to my feet. Their names were Alex and Jennifer. They called an ambulance for me and waited till it got there. I came to learn that Alex was the college captain, and Jennifer was his girlfriend. They walked home from school together every day as they lived close, and it was only twenty minutes.

Alex politely offered to accompany me to the hospital. I told him I would be fine and that I had some family that could meet me there. I only asked them to take my bike home.

We parted ways, but I will never forget that outstanding act of kindness. Sitting in the waiting room was a bore. Turns out suspected broken arms aren't on the list of priorities for doctors when people are coming in with serious injuries. It seems fair enough in hindsight, but it's never a fun wait when you're in pain. Mum was there in a heartbeat and sat by my side for five hours until we were seen. We drove home. I ran straight upstairs to my room and hid away for the next eight hours. It was nice to sit down and relax in the night time while everyone else was asleep, to relax in my serenity that I'd so badly craved all day. I never made it to school the next day nor the rest of the week. I didn't make it to football training, either. I wasn't leaving this place not now, not ever.

If I could write off that whole year, I would. The year was nothing but what's been described already. There weren't many highs, and every day was filled with lows. If I could ever give anyone advice, it's be you, be happy.

Late in September, our nation stood still for the most important game of the year, the Grand Final. It was a replay between the two best teams. The previous year only three points separated them in one of the most thrilling encounters. I couldn't have been any more excited to watch the game with my parents. My brother was out with his friends and my sister with hers. I thought it was just going to be Dad, Mum, and I, but Dad invited some new work friends and their families over. I didn't even get to watch the game. The team that had lost the previous year got their revenge by winning by two points. It was arguably the greatest grand final ever. I didn't even care, because Dad's boss bought his son along. A year older than me, and we caught on like a house on fire. We played video games from the start of the game right through till midnight. When it was time for them to go home, it didn't stop. We continued back at his house till early in the morning.

Mark's family lived closer to the city center, so our plans were to catch an early movie at the cinemas. After the movies, we had a goal to complete the games we were playing. Come Sunday evening, we lost the TV to Mark's sister as she wanted to watch her program. At first, I wasn't happy, but I stayed quiet while he argued with his parents about changing the channel. A young girl came running upstairs, and I was lost for breath. I had never seen someone so beautiful in my life.

"Aliyah, this is Brendan," Mark quickly stated. "Brendan, this is Aliyah."

Some moments never leave you. She wore a light-yellow dress, had blonde hair, and the most gorgeous smile I'd ever seen. Not one of us said a word to each other, we just stood there, gazes meeting in complete silence. I'll never forget seeing her for the first time. It was like that saying, the world stood still. I went home from Mark's later that night and went to bed, but for the first time in a long time, I didn't dread waking up for tomorrow. It was nice to have a reason to smile.

When I finally went back to school in eighth grade, seventh grade seemed like a dream. I'm not aware of how they randomly select the classes, but if everyone from that group of bullies could be put into one homeroom, they were. Every day the same group did the same shit. What I would have given to not exist. It would have been a dream, but instead, it felt like I had bright spotlights on me. To go from enjoying the comfort of your home for three months back to all that made the first week a grind.

The countdown had started for the next school holidays. Friday morning meant our first ever partial care. Partial care was our spare period and gave everyone some time to reflect and think about their futures, about how to approach them and the directions to take. Mr. Thomas was my homeroom teacher. He took us for sport, math and partial care. He sat next to me while everyone else brainstormed their ideas.

"Brendan, what do you want to be when you're older?" he asked.

I shrugged with not a glimmer of excitement nor a glimmer of enjoyment.

"Brendan," he sternly stated, "surely there is something you enjoy more than anything and want to do it for the rest of your life."

"I don't know," I replied.

I always knew, but why add fuel to a fire? Why give them something else to torment me about? It never occurred to me that my teachers would join the list of people trying to tear me down a few levels. Call them realists or call them assholes, aren't they supposed to encourage you to chase your dreams?

"Brendan, tell me."

The urgency in Mr. Thomas' voice was enough to draw any man's thoughts out of his mind, let alone a teenager.

"I-I-I . . . want . . . I want to play professional football," I responded in fear.

My fear was followed by regret as a wave of chuckles could be heard across the room. "Professional football?" he responded.

"Yes, sir."

"Well, let me tell you a thing or two about the pros," he began. "My son currently plays, and there are two kinds of players. Those with lots of talent and those with decent talent but work hard. You want to make it to the big league? Find a new ambition and stop wasting my time."

Our bravest moments come from sheer embarrassment. To sit there silently knowing the judgment and the repercussions to follow later, that's true strength.

In December, I decided it was time to take a trip home. It had been almost two years since the last time I set foot on soil in Western Australia. I've never understood the weather and how sometimes you have cloud coverage but no storms, or you can have very little clouds and a sun shower. Either way, we left the Melbourne airport in stormy conditions. I made the mistake of wearing Ugg boots, jeans, and a hoodie. The weather was fourteen degrees in Melbourne, yet four hours later it became sunny and thirty-eight degrees Celsius. The plane touched down at Perth airport without a cloud in the sky, and it was bloody hot, mind you. Nanna greeted me with a big kiss and a cuddle. We found my suitcase and hopped in the car for the hour and a half ride home, talking the whole time. The usual subjects came up, but no matter how much we talked, I was very mindful to keep to the basics.

Eventually, we arrived at what would be my new home for the next two months. The family were set to join us for Christmas but could only stay for a week due to work commitments. I was by myself for a few weeks, and I can't say I accomplished much other than enjoying the sun and computer games with food. It was two months of relaxing and caring about absolutely nothing. Eventually, though, my haven had to come to an end, and it was time to head back to Victoria to get on with life.

After four long hours, we touched down in Victoria. Dad and Mum tried to assure me they'd had reasonable weather while I was away, but I didn't believe them. It was as cloudy and as miserable as it had ever been, something that should never occur in late January. We grabbed my suitcase and proceeded to drive home. I talked to Dad and Mum the whole time. I did miss them dearly. They are the only two people who can genuinely make me smile, but that wasn't the case for that day. I knew I started school again in two days. I knew in two days my haven would become a distant memory. I walked inside and marched straight upstairs. No strut in my step, not even the slightest bit of joy. I felt lifeless. I was about to begin unpacking before I decided to have a shower.

The combination of the plane ride home and fast food had left me feeling dirty. While undressing in the mirror, I noticed something I had not noticed for two months. I had put on weight. I don't know if it was the specific lighting or the different mirrors from Nan's house to ours, but it was noticeable. I reluctantly mustered up the courage to weigh myself.

One-hundred kilograms, triple figures at thirteen years old. One-hundred kilograms. You know bullying has finally beaten you when you turn on yourself. How many thirteen-year old's do you know that's cracked the tonne? I was never proud of what followed next, but I was desperate to lose weight. When I pulled the glass door open, I turned on only the cold tap in the shower. I didn't feel comfortable with what I was about to do, but sometimes when people are desperate, desperate measures win out.

I proceeded to force myself to vomit. I didn't know much about it, but you hear those comments about models sticking their fingers down their throats. I did just that. I continued to vomit until I couldn't anymore, only taking breaks to squash the chunks of food down the shower drain.

Bulimia is a topic never really touched on in modern day society. I mean you do hear the jokes when models are mentioned and the rumors. It's never explained properly though. Bulimia is not a fun experience for anyone, but it was worse for me. I'll never forget that one day for many reasons. That day changed who I was completely. I had received my share of unwarranted beatdowns both physically and verbally, from people I love and from those who I had never really met before. I'd always managed to brush them off and retreat to my own little world. The main reason I will never forget that day is they were in my head. I had lost my innocence.

The next few months began to take their toll. My daily routine consisted of walking to and from school and trashing the lunch Mum had prepared for me. I was only consuming an apple for breakfast and some dinner. I managed to make a friend, though. Dylan was a funny kid, and it felt nice to finally have a friend. He took my mind off my daily grind, most of the time. His nickname for me was fatty. Although I really wasn't a fan of the nickname, I needed a friend. It's any wonder why high school can't be for everyone.

For three months straight, my life consisted of waking up at seven, going to school, doing my homework on the bus, to footy training, and then training, before going home, eating dinner, and falling asleep. I would repeat the same process every day. It was routine work with nothing to get excited about. Eventually, though, I received my first compliment in many years. I was walking across the footy oval to sit with Dylan. He was with two guys named Jacob and Peter. As well as three girls Alison, Lisa, and Steph. I was joining them for lunch.

Dylan laughed before he began. "You know we actually didn't recognize who you were from the other side of the oval. How much weight have you lost? You look so different, man."

Internally, I was ecstatic. Externally, I tried not to show. "I'm not sure, mate. Just trying to eat a little healthier."

Truth is I knew. The truth is I was obsessed. I'd weigh myself three times a day as a minimum. I'd lost thirty kilograms in under three months, but I wasn't going to admit it to anyone.

"Sure, I'm still going to call you fatty, ya fatty," he replied.

Football season began not long after, and it was a lot easier to play now that I had slimmed down. I knew my habit didn't help with training, so I kicked the habit quickly. For something that had been so routine and so automatic, it surprised me how easily I could part ways with what had been such an obsession for so long. It was a nice feeling not having that black cloud over my head. Whenever I'd vomited, my body had filled up with anger and hatred, like what adrenaline does to your body when you work out. I guess that's what subconsciously convinced me to quit. I just wanted to feel happy. The most surprising part about being skinny and athletic is the friends you suddenly have. Everyone seems to love you. No one knows what you went through, and no one cares. Those people are fake friends.

They were the same people who stole my phone in year seven. The same people who used to beat me up. The same people who always made me feel like an outcast. They were never worthy of my time, but it was easier to keep on their good side rather than their bad. A huge shock to me, though, was my teammates. With being skinny, my football talent vastly improved, and that meant they wanted to be my friend. I'm not talking about the passing joke in the schoolyard or having a kick before school. I mean catching up on the weekend and playing video games together. That sort of friend.

It felt nice to be liked, and I was riding on a cloud. It seemed like this was my year, and I wasn't going to let it go. All that hard work, the struggles, and regret. It was all gone. It's interesting how my outlook on life could change so instantly. My outlook was positive, and I was never seen without a smile. My life kept moving upwards even to the point of being named captain.

The season started, and we had won our first four games. It was round five, and we had a matchup for the top spot. I was playing on the best center half forward in the competition. We lead for the ball, but it had dropped short and bounced past us. I went to turn around, and I received a strong bump from my opposing player. I lost my balance at full speed. To this day, I can still remember the pain from both the side of my foot and my ankle touching the ground at the same time. I was helped off the field by both the runners and taken straight to emergency where I waited with Mum.

"Are you nervous?" she asked.

"Nope, but this wait isn't helping."

"How come you aren't nervous?" she asked with a queried look.

"I know it's broken. I could tell when it happened."

Mum patted me on the leg. "Hopefully it won't leave you on the sidelines for too long."

Having Mum with me waiting around for six hours was nice. Dad joined us after the game had finished, and we just passed time while clock watching.

A man appeared from behind a door. "Brendan," he called loudly in a questioning tone, but he wasn't demanding.

We followed the gentlemen down the hall to the room to be examined. "I'm doctor Klose," he expressed "And you are?" he asked Dad as he shook his hand.

"Bill," Dad responded.

"And?" Doctor Klose gestured to Mum as he shook her hand.

"Sam."

"Nice to meet you. Now Brendan, how about you hop up onto the bed and show me your injury."

I struggled onto the bed. Doctor Klose and Dad helped me out. He started fiddling with my ankle.

Yes, very swollen, what happened?"

"I was running and went to switch direction. As I did, I was bumped, and I felt the side of my foot and my ankle touch the ground at the same time."

"That sounds very painful," he responded.

I nodded at doctor Klose, wincing in pain as felt around the swollen area.

"It looked very painful," Mum added.

"Well, from your description and the swelling around the ankle we will order some x-rays and go from there."

We took some x-rays before heading home to sleep. I was exhausted, but I didn't sleep at all that night, not because of the pain. I couldn't switch my mind off. I was too busy hoping it wasn't broken. After eventually catching a few hours of shut-eye, I awoke the next morning to the phone ringing. It was Doctor Klose with my results.

"Hey, Brendan the news isn't good. There's a break in your ankle. How soon can you come in to get your leg put in a cast?"

The next six months, I can't say I was as bored as I expected to be. It was nice to relax in my room again, but the weight added on fast. One thing I noticed as I began to put on weight was how people change. Those fake friends I told you about earlier, the jokes in the schoolyard, the kicking of the football before school, that all disappeared. I became their jokes again. When Dylan called me fatty, it began to hurt again. I started to become that hermit who hated school and had a real negative outlook on life. After the two months were up it was time to take the cast off and begin rehabilitation. Walking was a bitch. You never appreciate your body while everything works like it's supposed too but try walking every day in agony. Try getting out of bed every morning and bearing all your weight on your injury. The next year was a struggle.

CHAPTER THREE: A DIRE NEED FOR HELP

I remember slowly waking my eyes to the clock. Tick, tock, tick, tock. It was ten in the morning, and I lay there motionless, peaceful, with not an ounce of movement overcoming my body.

I heard faintly, "Patient is about six feet in height and looks malnourished, no fat on face. He has short, brown messy hair and is sixteen years of age."

The hospital bed was raised from my torso up, and the room was pure white along with my gown. There was a window above my head that was supposed to let in the sun, but there was no sunshine. Just dark-thick-grey-clouds.

There was also a viewing window beyond my feet where two doctors were standing with clipboards in hand. One, a woman with long brunette hair pinned back in a ponytail, had black spectacles on and stood around five-foot-six-inches with her black heels on. She wore black slacks and a white doctors coat over the top that read: "Gibbins, M.D." The other, a young Asian male, wore a stethoscope around his neck. He had short black hair and was wearing a dress shirt, slacks, and polished black shoes.

I slowly came to as they opened the door.

"Hi, Brendan. How are you feeling?" asked Doctor Gibbins,

"Confused and lost, a little bit scared to be honest," I replied.

"Well, Brendan, I'm Doctor Sally Gibbins, and this is Doctor Thomas Chang. Doctor. Chang is a student." Sally Gestured to her left to where Doctor Chang was standing at the end of the bed.

"He is currently still studying. I hope you don't mind a student doctor in the room?"

"I-I guess not," I hesitantly responded. "We all have to learn somewhere." As I spoke, I had a wincing grin over my face. I was trying to make jokes to feel comfortable, but it was obvious that I was scared.

"Well, it's morning time, and we would like to see you get some food into you. You don't look too healthy, and I'm sure you're starving after being asleep for so long."

I glanced at Doctor Gibbins shyly before looking towards the bowl of cereal placed in front of me. Drenched in fear, I raised my head towards Doctor Gibbins.

"Brendan," said Doctor Gibbins, her voice deeper and stern, a lot more serious than how the conversation original-ly started. "We would like to see you eat."

I pushed the bowl to the side and looked up to her. "I'm sorry, Doctor Gibbins. I'm just not hungry."

"Not hungry? Or not able to eat?"

Surprised by her remark, I gazed upon the bowl of cereal. My fear had been overcome by despair.

"Brendan, are you hungry? Or not?" she asked.

I cut Doctor Gibbins off with a swift, yet eager reply. "Don't make me answer that one. All of us know the response."

I've never felt so ashamed in my life. My dirty secret had come to light. I bowed my head and looked at my tummy in shame. A single tear fell from my left eye and slid rapidly down my cheek before I began to sob uncontrollably. I tried my best to hold it all together not moving, not making eye contact with anyone in the room, just keeping my head bowed towards my tummy.

"I would like to evaluate you further, if this is okay with

you? We took the liberty of booking you in for a one o'clock appointment with Thomas and myself. You need help, and we would like to try our best."

I never raised my head. I just nodded, tears still streaming down my cheeks.

"Rest up and we will see you in a few hours. Your family is here and would love to see how you are doing."

Doctor Gibbins and Doctor Chang both exited the room before I was greeted by my mother and father. They gently embraced me and didn't say a word.

It was one in the afternoon. I slowly made my way down the halls of the hospital. I didn't have the slightest spring in my step, let alone any urgency. My face was bowed towards the ground, my shoulders slumped, and I reeked. Not of smell, but rather of disappointment and a defeated attitude. I entered a room on the lowest floor of the hospital, two floors below the ground. Doctor Chang and Doctor Gibbins waited for me.

"Come in, Brendan, have a seat," Doctor Gibbins gestured to the chair on the other side of the table from where they sat.

The room wasn't inviting. The bottom of the hospital was in the process of being renovated, which didn't help the situation. The room was painted dark grey with patches of white from where the painters had started but were yet to finish. There were no windows, just a table in the center of the room and a camera on a tripod in between the doctors, angled down towards the empty chair waiting for me. The dimly lit overhead light flickered. It was time for a new globe.

"Do you mind if we film this session, Brendan?" queried Doctor Chang. "We like to re-watch our tapes to identify important information we may have missed throughout the session."

I nodded.

Doctor Gibbins began to speak, "Well, Brendan, first off we want to explain to you why we bought you here. All we ask is you answer every question with complete honesty. After your fall, during physical education, we did some enquiring as it is rare for a young man like yourself, who is in very good shape, to collapse during physical activity. We have been in contact with the health and well-being officer, Tate Presani, from your school. She informs us you that have been talking and exploring ideas on how to conquer bulimia. Bulimia is a serious condition that varies from person to person. Whether it be minor or severe, the treatment can be a long and strenuous road. Can you begin by explaining to us why you wouldn't eat your breakfast this morning?"

"I can't eat food anymore unless it's late at night, but generally I feel too unwell to eat then, too," I replied. I spoke from sheer guilt, sure they could hear the despair sweep through my voice from the second my mouth opened.

"When you say you can't eat food anymore what do you mean?" Doctor Gibbins asked.

"I-I . . ." I paused for a moment and took a deep breath before gathering myself and continuing. "When it first started, it was forced by me. After the odd meal, I would take a shower and force myself to be ill. Now whenever I eat, I vomit. I can't control it anymore. Even just looking at food has the tendency to make me sick."

"How do you feel when you vomit?" asked Doctor Gibbins.

"Helpless." I didn't hesitate to answer, nor did I question my answer for even a second. Nor did I avoid eye contact with either doctor. They could tell from the hasty response that I hated this feeling, but I had felt it many times before.

"Helpless?" Doctor Chang questioned with the most puzzled look on his face. "What do you mean?"

"I don't know. I just know I'm not in control, and I hate it. I really do."

Doctor Gibbins finished the line she was writing. She dropped her pen, clasped her hands together and placed them on the table. She looked directly at me. "Well, Brendan, the stage of bulimia you are currently experiencing stems from sub-conscious triggers. Over an extended time of forcing yourself to vomit, your body's natural reflexes have kicked in. It's like blinking or even breathing."

I looked at her in confusion. "Is it easy to fix?" I asked.

"Depends on the person," she replied. "Your program will be long. We will first try our best to get to the bottom of the psychological side of the problems. Each person will have their own different routines that will suit them. We could find yours within a day or it could take a few months, maybe even a year."

After listening intently, I nodded. I understood every word they said.

It was agreed after a week at the hospital that they didn't understand the condition enough to continue. They identified the best rehabilitation center for me to attend. I was discharged from the hospital and sent straight there. I walked inside for the first time to a vibrant building with vibrant surroundings.

A lady approached us. "Welcome, Brendan. We have been expecting you. How are you today?"

"I'm a little taken back. This is such a bright place," I responded.

"We find the majority of our patients do their healing in a bright and fun atmosphere. They come to us confused and lost, and we take pride in treating their conditions, so they feel positive about their lives again. It starts with a positive room. What were you expecting?"

I smiled, as I knew it would be a nice change to be surrounded by the bright blue, green, and pink walls, rather than the dark charcoal I had been around for the last four years at school.

"Honestly, I was expecting something like a hospital," I replied.

"As much as they serve quite similar purposes, you'll realize the different ends of the spectrum that we're on. I'll let Leroy here show you to your room. How about the four of us meet back in half an hour for some lunch? There I can show you around the facilities and help you get settled."

I smiled as Leroy led Dad, Mum, and me down the corridor to my room. The room was a very white, very neutral setting. There was a single bed either side of the door and a window at the other end of the room covered in fauna. At the foot of each of the beds lay two drawers. Leroy left us alone to settle in. Dad and Mum sat on the bed while I unpacked some of my clothes.

"It's a nice spot here," Mum began. "Do you really think the change of environment will help?"

I didn't say anything. I just smiled. I wasn't sure, but I had hoped it would.

"You know we can find help closer to home?" Mum teared up as Dad put his hand around her shoulder. I could see her starting to sob, although she tried desperately to hide it.

"It's just that two and a half hours is a long way, and we will only get to see you on weekends."

I walked over and took Mum's outstretched arm before sitting on the bed between them. I put my arms around their shoulders and pulled them into my chest. "I need this. It's only temporary, a couple of weeks at most, I promise." All three of us sat there for what felt like an hour, embraced in each other's arms. None of us spoke until there was a knock at the door. It was the lady from the beginning.

"Are you guys ready to grab that lunch?" she asked. We all stood up and followed her down the hall.

"I should actually introduce myself. My name is Jane Myers, I am your appointed counsellor."

She paused for a second as we exchanged greetings, each shaking her hand.

She continued. "This institute has an impressively high success rate." We walked into another room. "This is the lounge room. It's full of gaming consoles, books, and TV's. We find a great way to help with the rehabilitation process is to bond with others sharing struggles of their own."

We continued to walk down the hall to a kitchen.

"We daily prepare every meal that you choose. Everyone chooses where they want to eat. They can be seated in the dining hall." She gestured to her left to a little room with a table in the middle of it. The table had eight chairs around it and looked like it also doubled as a staff room. "Patients may also like the privacy of eating in their rooms or eating in the tranquil gardens outside. Whatever feels most comfortable is what we preach. Some patients . . ." She nodded at me.

" . . . are required to eat with their counselor or have a representative present at meal times, not necessarily to ensure the food is eaten but to document their habits and best tailor a solution to these problems."

"Yeah, that makes sense. Some people might be uneasy about it. I'm not embarrassed or trying to hide it. I just want help." I responded.

Counsellor Myers smiled. "Along with scheduled classes to keep their education up, you will be required to meet with me once a day as a check up on your healing progress. Other than those rules, patients can do as they please within the facilities. At the end of the day, this is not forced upon you, but a chance to heal in a positive environment. Did you have any questions?"

Before I had a chance to ask any questions I possessed, Mum jumped in with asking about visitation policies.

"Good question, Samantha," Counsellor Myers responded.

"We don't have policies for some as they need love and support, but some patients do require a complete break from the outside world and their family. We ask you don't visit or call for four days. By then, we can understand the triggers in each patient and whether they can heal properly with the outside world around."

Counsellor Myers paused for a few moments. She could see the heartbreak in Mum's eyes. I could feel it. I was heart-broken, too.

"Are there any other questions?" Counsellor Myers asked.

I turned to my right to see Dad. He seemed upset but understood. I looked to my left to see Mum. She was trying to choke back sobs.

"There doesn't seem to be any at this stage," I told her. "That I can think of, anyway."

"I will let you guys spend some time together while I go sort out your schedule."

Counsellor Myers walked back inside while Dad, Mum, and I all went for a wander. The gardens were beautiful, and they seemed endless. The colors of the arrangements were very peaceful. Water fountains with lots of green foliage, while light blue, pink, and white flowers all surrounded the foliage created a garden of water trickling and birds chirping. It was magical. I walked over and picked two roses, a white one for Dad and a pink one for Mum. I smiled to Mum and Dad. They smiled back.

As I handed them the roses, Mum spoke up. "Promise me you will be home before they die."

"But mu —" I didn't finish my words.

Dad had cut me off. "Promise," he added.

I was left speechless, so I nodded. I knew it wasn't true but sometimes others needed to hear what they wanted, regardless of the truth. We walked over and sat on a different bench to pass time. The bench faced west. We got to witness the sun set perfectly over the water fountain and green hedges. Dad sat back with his foot on his other knee and his arms around the back of the chair whilst Mum rested her head on my shoulder. None of us said a word. We just enjoyed the sunset.

Eventually, it came time for Mum and Dad to leave. After a very long goodbye, I made my way into my room to finish unpacking. While I was in the middle of folding my clothes, a boy made his way into my room. He looked young, late teens, but had the stature of a fully-grown man. His presence was noted immediately.

"You must be the new guy." He grinned. "I'm Jesse," he said as he stretched out his hand.

I shook his hand. "Pleasure, mate. I'm Brendan."

Jesse lay down on his bed while I continued to unpack. He clasped his hands and rested his head on them. He was a unit, easily six-foot-two with black hair, and I could tell he was a gym regular. He also had a black spacer in each ear. He was cool, popular, oozed confidence, but he was down to Earth and not arrogant at all.

"So where are you from?" he asked.

"*Geelong*," I replied hastily, without making any eye contact.

"Ahhh." He paused for a moment before finishing. "The greatest team of all."

Although I had my back turned to him, I smiled. "Yeah, apparently."

"Brothers, sisters?" he asked,

"One and one, both older."

"Hobbies?"

"Any sports, mate. I'm not fussed."

Jesse grinned as he answered. "Yeah me, too."

I'm never normally blatantly short with people, but there was something about Jesse that threw me on guard. I knew not to get to close to the confident ones, regardless of their situation.

"You're not too talkative, are ya?" he asked.

I shook my head.

Jesse sat up and put his back against the wall. "Why are you here, mate?"

I was stumped by that question. Maybe I misunderstood the treatment facility. I turned to face Jesse. "Aren't we all here for the same thing?" I questioned.

"Not at all. You will quickly learn the difference."

That comment left me with many unanswered questions. It wasn't a passing comment. He was right. That's why I was there. I didn't know much about the condition I had. I just know I wanted help.

"Want to come play the console?" he asked.

"Of course, but I haven't played in a while."

"No stress, mate. We'll start a new game."

We headed down the hall to the recreation room. It was nine-thirty at night. I was quite surprised there was no curfew. Maybe the other patients enjoyed a bit of freedom. Maybe the centre knew they were all early sleepers. I wasn't sure. It was nice to be the only ones in the recreation room. Around eleven-thirty, we called it a night. Not a bad first day at all.

We woke up to Jesse's alarm at eight-thirty. It was gangster's paradise by Coolio. Jesse looked at me and laughed.

"It's always fun to wake up to that. It soothes me," Jesse

said.

I laughed with him as he went to turn off the alarm.

"Nah, mate, don't do that," I said as I sat up from the bed.

Jesse just looking at me. He stood up on his bed, crossed his arms with his chin in the air, then bent down and flexed his arms with his fingers shaped like a gun. While looking at me in the traditional rapper pose, he began to shout the lyrics.

The door flew open. It was Counsellor Myers.

"Great first day I see, Brendan, in trouble before breakfast." She smiled. "On a serious note, it's nice to see you both getting along so well. Just try to keep it down a little bit, please."

Counsellor Myers closed the door. Jesse and I looked at each other as the door opened again. "And get off the beds!" Counsellor Myers ordered.

We both hopped down. Jesse had a nine o'clock meeting. I put my headphones on and wandered around for some time. The music calmed me. The garden was surprisingly large, and it was a beautiful morning, predominantly blue skies with sunshine. I saw a few butterflies flying and hoped that they would be a frequent occurrence. Truth be told, though, I wondered whether it seemed better because of how nervous I was, or whether every room was more beautiful because it wasn't the counselor's office? It was my first meeting. I didn't know what to expect.

Time was up, and I was ready to head to Counsellor Myers' office. I walked in and took a seat on the black leather armchair. Her office smelt fresh, like everything had been bought that morning. It was certainly interesting. The rest of the facility had bright and vibrant colors, but this office was very dull. I immediately felt a change in the atmosphere like the office meant business.

"How are you, Brendan?" she asked.

"Good." I paused for a moment. "Nervous," I added.

"Why?" Counsellor Myers responded. "You seemed to be having so much fun this morning."

"This is a bright facility with bright colors everywhere. The people so far seem very friendly. It's also a place of healing, and I don't quite understand what that entails. If this room is anything to go by, it's serious."

"The room is designed to make the patient feel slightly uncomfortable. We must find your trigger points to develop a successful rehabilitation program. The dullness is supposed to shock the system. Then you leave into happy brighter hallways."

"You subconsciously play tricks?" I asked.

"Not necessarily tricks, but a lot of our patients are very guarded. Sometimes we need to reach the information to help heal. By the way, you're the first person to ever query that." Counsellor Myers paused for a moment with a stunned look on her face. "Have you always been that observant?"

I couldn't tell you why she was asking. All I can tell is that her face went from surprised and confused to relieved. It's hard to explain, but it was like a light bulb went off in her head. Like she had a theory and was very curious to hear my response.

"I don't really remember. I've always been quiet in any room I've been in. I just listen to any information at hand." I paused for a moment. I was curious. I didn't know what the counselor was digging for, but I wanted to remain guarded until I figured it out.

"You sit there quietly observing everything?" she asked.

"Yes."

"Okay." Counsellor took a deep breath. It seemed like she was very nervous to continue speaking.

"Tell me, were you or are you currently being bullied?"

I nodded.

"When you observe, do you observe people's conversations?"

I nodded again.

Counsellor Myers had lost her curious look like she had found what she was looking for.

"Have you ever used these conversations against others?"

"Maybe a few times. I have never really felt the need to."

"But you would?" She asked.

Now I had to have had the blankest look on my face. I didn't understand in the slightest.

"Would you use what you've heard to hurt others?"

"Well, not intentionally. I've always known what would upset someone the most, but I don't like hurting others. They would have to do something pretty bad."

"It's a defense mechanism," she stated.

"Pardon?" I asked.

"You're keeping your cards close to your chest. Most people would never be so guarded yet so observant. Personally, I think it comes from bullying. No one tries to protect themselves when they don't need protecting."

I didn't disagree. That made sense, although I never consciously did it.

"It's only your first session," Counsellor Myers continued. "Don't stress too much. We won't go too much further. I hope you don't remain so guarded towards me and can open up in due time." She put down her notepad and removed her glasses. "All that's left for me to do is to shadow you while you eat breakfast. From the report I received from Doctor Gibbins, I believe you enjoy cereal."

I nodded at her, and we both stood up. She gestured to the door. "Shall we?" she asked.

We left her office and walked down the hall to the kitchen. The cereal and the bowl were in front of me, and I grabbed the milk out of the fridge. I poured the milk into the bowl before picking the bowl up.

"You're welcome to eat wherever you feel most comfortable," she said.

"Honestly, the dining room would be best, if it's free?" I rhetorically asked.

We walked down the hall a few mere meters to see if the dining hall was free. She pretended not to be there as she stood behind me against the wall. My first few mouthfuls went down a treat, but it's a weird feeling having someone watch you eat. I picked my bowl up, walked around the table, and sat on the opposite side facing her.

"When did you get into this business?" I asked.

I know it was very cliché small talk, but I didn't know where to start.

"My sister, actually, she struggled a lot with body image and anorexia, so I wanted to help people who are lost."

You always assume anyone in this business wants to help people, but having it affect loved ones closer to them was surprising. "How's your sister today?" I asked.

A look of despair swept across Counsellor Myers' face. At this stage, I knew I had asked too much.

"How about we just focus on you?"

I felt so bad, I kept my head down, staring at my breakfast. I finished fast and put my spoon down.

"Quick eater I see," Counsellor Myers said. I nodded and smiled. "What happens next?" she asked.

"I generally go for a shower."

We proceeded down the vacant halls to the bathroom. I leaned up against the wall facing the sink with my arms folded. Counsellor Myers stared at me.

"So?" she asked.

"We wait a few minutes," I replied.

"You don't force this upon yourself?" she asked.

I shook my head.

"That's very interesting."

The rest of the day seemed like a blur. The days rolled into weeks, and the weeks went very fast. I wasn't nervous, though. I trusted Counsellor Myers. Knowing this had affected someone so close to her gave me a lot of faith that she could help me. I didn't sleep the night though, not for fear or regret or even sadness It was excitement more than anything. I was excited to be done with being tired and excited to be done with hating myself. I was ready to be happy.

The morning started like any other in that place. I woke up and went for a walk in the garden, sat by the fountain, and enjoyed the sunrise. Ten o'clock came around very quickly, and it was time for my meeting. I was excited. After only a few short weeks, it already felt like serious progress.

"How are you today?" she asked.

"I'm all right. Excited." I paused, "Hoping I can go home very soon."

"That's pleasing to hear. I want to try a new method today. I'm really hoping it might work, but if it does, it can possibly lead to other complications."

I smiled, "Let's do it. That's an eighter job."

Counsellor Myers stared at me with the blankest look on her face. I knew she didn't get it. She asked, "What's an eighter job?"

"It's a joke for later. If this fixes the problem, we can deal with the rest later."

The look on counselor's face was priceless, like she had never heard a lamer joke in her life. "Anyway, ah, let's move on and pretend that never happened. I want you to mix your day up a little bit, your days are so routine, your body has adapted to it. You're not having any fun. Personally, I believe your body became so used to the reaction after food, your mind made your bathroom time after eating an automatic response. Let's change that today. We will go for a walk after breakfast, try break that habit."

We proceeded to head down to the dining room.

"You're eating faster than usual," she stated.

"I'm excited. I really hope this works." I responded.

"Me, too."

After I finished, we went on our walk through the gardens. "You've been here three weeks. Did you expect to ever be here this long?" she asked.

"To be honest, I'm not sure. This issue has been going on for months. I had high hopes of only being here a few days, but a lot of me thought it was going to be a few months at least. I was completely in limbo, and after hearing how long some of the patients had been here, it didn't give me much confidence."

"You're not wrong."

"How long did you think I would be here, Counsellor?" I asked.

"I was never sure. From day one you had a unique condition, so to speak. We thought your condition was more medical and that our facilities couldn't cater to your condition, but I saw something in you that made me smile."

"What was that?"

"I spend a lot of my day treating those who are forced to be here. As a counselor, every now and then you get a person who genuinely wants to help themselves. You cling to them like crazy because it's rarer than you think." Counselor stopped for a moment, seemingly to gather her thoughts. "I may not see another you for years."

I nodded. I was stunned, I genuinely didn't know how to respond to that.

"How are you feeling by the way?" Counsellor asked.

"Great. Why?"

"It's been twenty minutes."

"Oh, wow, I didn't even realise."

"It's just about breaking up the mental cycle. Let's switch it up from now on. Go for a small walk after every time you eat, and hopefully it will work."

The rest of my day was very simple. I took some time to lie on my bed and reflect. Counsellor Myers was right. My life had become so routine, so mundane, what was I ever excited for? My days were the same. I never smiled. It was predictable.

The day had been a shock to the system. I was alive, but I wasn't living. My ten o'clock appointment came around. I sat in the black leather armchair like usual.

"Didn't get much sleep last night, did you?" Counsellor asked.

Truth was I didn't. I couldn't. I had too much on my mind.

"Today I want to talk to you about depression." Counsellor began. "Do you know much about depression?"

I knew a lot. I was very interested to see where this was going. "Very basic knowledge," I responded.

"Okay, I would like you to see a friend of mine. She specializes in it, and I believe you show some symptoms."

"Why?" I was very defensive. I believed it was a term everyone threw around.

"Because you've been taking beatings. Mentally, physically, and verbally for a very long time now. The effects are evident."

"I'm not depressed, Counsellor," I responded.

"I think you are. All you do is hide from people. You're scared at times to go to school or football due to ridicule, and you developed an extremely unhealthy condition which has taken you to an unhealthy physical and mental state. Tell me you're happy."

I had tears in my eyes at that stage. "I appreciate everything you have done for me. I will never be able to fully express how grateful I am." I stood up to leave.

"Sit down," Counsellor ordered.

"No!"

"You need help".

"I'm not depressed. I agreed to come here because I needed help. I can admit when I need it."

"You do need help. Why don't you believe that you're depressed?"

At that stage, tears were streaming down my face. "I've watched people close to me go through years of depression. Not having the ability to get out of bed, sitting alone at night in a dark room by themselves. They never talked about it much. Although one quote from my uncle always stood out. He told me depression is like one day you're driving. It's a sunny day, and you enter a dark tunnel. No matter how fast you drive, no matter how much you want too, you can't find the light. You want to get out of the darkness, but with no end in sight, you question whether you ever will, whether you will be in this darkness forever. The more time you spend in this tunnel, the more the darkness becomes your reality. As for me, there was no sunny day, there were no smiles. I started in the tunnel, but I can see the light, and I know I'll eventually get there. This tunnel might be three kilometers long, but every day I take a step closer to happiness. It'll take its time, but I'll get there, and I'll be happy."

Counsellor didn't say a word. She didn't have anything to say. I opened the door, but before I left, I turned to face her. "Give me a reason to smile, and I'll show you the biggest one you've ever seen."

I shut the door behind me and walked straight to the phone at the end of the corridor. "Mum, can you please come pick me up? I'm ready."

I proceeded to my room and packed my things. Counselor greeted me at my door. She didn't say a word. She was just speechless. I gave her a hug. She didn't hug me back.

"I'll forever be in your debt. Thank you," I said.

Counsellor Myers smiled. "Take care of yourself, Brendan."

Mum gave me the biggest hug in the world. It had been too long since we had seen each other. She was very teary. I would have been, too, but after no sleep and a roller coaster of emotions, I was mentally drained. We hopped in the car and began our journey home.

"Why are you coming home?" Mum asked.

"I'm just ready."

"You know I love you, Brendan?"

"I love you too, Mum."

"Why are you coming home?"

"Can't you just be happy?"

"Trust me, I am happy, but I spoke to you two days ago, and you weren't ready." Mum took a deep breath. "And Counsellor Myers didn't look happy. What happened?"

"She thinks I'm depressed."

Mum looked at me. "So?" She questioned why that mattered as if she agreed.

"I'm not depressed."

"You know there are certain levels of depression? Right?" Mum asked, but it seemed more rhetorical.

"I know, Mum, but I'll be happy one day. I promise."

There was a long pause. "Okay, as long as you think you're ready."

After about fifteen minutes, mum broke the silence. "School starts in a few days. Reckon you might go?"

"I'm unsure. I really want to."

"Whenever you're ready. No pressure."

When we arrived home, I went straight to my room. It was still the same except for the fact my keyboard was covered in dust. I collapsed on my bed and spread my arms and legs as if I was making a snow angel. There was so much more room after going from a single bed to a double. I woke up three hours later. I don't remember drifting off. I walked downstairs to see Mum slaving away making her famous pasta salad. Something delicious had caught my nostrils, a smell I had not smelled in quite some time.

"Morning, sleepy head," she joked.

"What are you doing?"

"Cooking," Mum swiftly replied.

"What are you cooking?" Before Mum could answer, I put my index finger up. "Wait." I sniffed the air as if I were trying to pick up a scent in the forest. My nose was high in the air taking short breathes.

"Lasagne?" I asked, although I knew I was right. The questioning look that had to be on my face was overcome with a smile.

"I wanted to cook you your favorite meal to say welcome home." Mum almost teared up.

"What's with the salads?" I asked.

"Oh, nothing really. It's just a little bit hot now, so I wanted to put something in the fridge for lunch."

"Mum."

"Yes, Brendan?"

"What's with the salads?" I asked again.

"I'm being honest," she replied

"I can tell you're lying, Mum. What's with the salads?"

"We bought a heap of ingredients for a BBQ at the Smith's, but now that you're home, we want to stay home. Rather than letting them go to waste, I thought I could make them up."

"Go to the barby, you goose," I demanded, jokingly.

At that stage, Mum was mixing the dressing into the salads with a wooden spoon.

"No! Not happening," she said sternly but with a smile.

"Mum, go to the barbecue."

Mum put down the wooden spoon and stared straight at me. With hesitation in her voice, she smiled. "You should come. It will be good for you."

"Nah, I'm all good, I just want to be alone." I turned around to walk upstairs to begin unpacking my gear.

"Aliyah will be there."

I smiled like an idiot, but none the less I didn't turn around. "I guess I better go get changed then, shouldn't I?"

We arrived at the Smith's house to see Aliyah dressed in a light blue dress with white polka dots. She wore white flat sneakers, and her long blonde hair was slicked back in a pony tail. Her lips were very shiny as they were covered in gloss, and her eyes were ever so beautiful—I could get lost in them forever. The reason I'll never forget that moment was it was the day I started looking at her as the girl I desired. She smiled at me as I walked in and gave me a hug.

"You look amazing," she told me.

I couldn't help grinning like an idiot. "As do you." "

"How was your holiday?" she asked.

My parents had told everyone I went to see family in Western Australia over the break.

"Yeah, all right, bit of sun but nothing special. What about yourself? What did you get up to over summer?"

We ended up talking for a good few hours before our parents decided it was time to head home. I wrapped my arms around Aliyah before I left.

"I'll see you soon, I hope," I said.

Aliyah didn't move or say anything. She just smiled, a smile so pure, I still smile when I remember it.

CHAPTER FOUR: A REASON TO SMILE

The next day I woke up smiling. I grabbed my suitcase and unpacked all my gear. I even rearranged my room. That day flew by, and it felt good to be home. I had Aliyah on my mind all day, and I decided to message her and ask her how her day went. We ended up talking on video chat till three in the morning. Although I had been around her house while visiting her brother, Mark, we had never had a full conversation. We had so much to talk about and catch up on. Even the smallest things, like how her favorite food is simply an apple. I know it was weird, but it intrigued me so much to find out about her. I had never felt this way before, and I wasn't sure if she felt the same way. It didn't mean I couldn't enjoy those feelings.

We kept talking over the next few nights and even when we went back to school. Staying up till three in the morning and then going to school was a task and a half. It was worth it, every single second. I finally mustered up enough courage to ask her out. It was a Friday night and we were on video, talking like usual. She agreed. We met at a causal Italian restaurant down on the waterfront. She looked stunning in her jeans, black top, and black boots.

"How are you feeling today?" I asked, grinning from ear to ear.

"I'm very tired." We both laughed at her response. "I feel like all I did was sleep today," she continued.

"Me, too," I replied. "No matter how much I slept, it wasn't enough."

Aliyah smiled as I spoke. I could tell she agreed. We took our seats at the restaurant on opposite sides of the small table.

"Does Mark know about this?" I asked.

Aliyah remained quiet.

"I haven't said a word yet. Have you?" I asked.

"Nah, I'm too scared to," she replied.

"If this becomes something, that's totally your job." I snickered while pouring two glasses of water.

"No, be a man. It's your job."

"Not a chance. He's more likely to be nicer to you. You're his sister. He can't stop loving you. I'm only the friend."

"Maybe we will do it together."

"Maybe."

I smiled.

The conversation started off a little slow, the usual small talk like how's school, how was your day, how's the family. But in no time, it was like no one else in the world existed. I truly mean that. Neither of us even saw the waitress walk over to our table.

"Hey, guys," the waitress said. We both jumped.

"Oh, wow I didn't see you sneak up on us," I said.

"I'm so sorry," she replied.

"Don't stress," said Aliyah.

"My name is Jess. I will be your waitress for tonight. Would you like to read the specials? Or are you guys ready to order?"

"I'm pretty good. I've been craving a pizza all day. Do you want time to read the menu?" I asked Aliyah.

"Nah, I'm fine I've been told the gnocchi here is amazing. I'll just go with that."

We both closed the menus and handed them to jess.

"Any drinks?" Jess asked.

"I'm happy with the water. Did you want anything?" I

asked.

"Nah, water will do just fine."

Jess walked away to process our orders. Aliyah turned to me. "What?" she asked, followed by a moment's pause. "What?" she repeated. "Why are you smiling?"

I didn't say anything.

"Brendan, answer me," she demanded.

"I just think it's awesome you're not getting a salad. It's like my favorite thing ever. I just assumed for all the dancing, it left you strict about your diet." I back-peddled a little bit. "Not that gnocchi is a bad meal. I just . . . mean that . . ."

Aliyah cut off my pregnant pauses. "Stop stressing. I know what you meant. I assume your description of a dancer comes from what the media and movies portray. I bloody love food. It's the best thing ever."

Our food came out, and we ate. Maybe the fact it was our first date made it all the sweeter. It made me wonder whether food tasted better dependent on the company you're with.

After eating, we walked along the beach and truly enjoyed a rare summer's sunset over the bay. It's hard to explain, but the sky lit up in a pink color and even colored the clouds. It was spectacular. Once the sun went down, we sat atop of Stateham's hill down by the water. Stateham' hill was in a great location. Once the sun went down, you could see all the night lights across the bay. You also got to see all the pretty lights from the central business district.

"It's truly romantic, isn't it?" Aliyah pointed to the city lights.

I leant in and kissed her. It could not have been better timing. To see the city, at night, from that spot was truly breathtaking, but it was the company I preferred. To share memories with someone who, surprisingly at that stage, meant so much more to me than she could understand. That's what made my night.

"I really like you." It was random and out of the blue, but she needed to know.

She always told me for many years after that it wasn't a coherent sentence. That it came in parts with a lot of stuttering. She remembers me being nervous and cute. All I remember is her smile.

"I really like you, too," she replied with the smile she tried to hide while staring at the ground.

"What happens next?" I asked.

"You could ask me to be your girlfriend."

"Not a bad idea, I like that."

"Me, too."

After Aliyah spoke, we sat there in silence. After about a minute she looked straight at me.

"Well?" she asked.

"Well what?" I responded.

"Are you going to ask me?"

"Probably not." I was laughing. "I've reconsidered," I jokingly announced.

Aliyah hit me playfully on the shoulder. "That's not nice," she said.

I took her by the hands and turned to the side to face her.

"I've always had a crush on you because of how pretty you are, but this last week I've really gotten to know you. You're the sweetest, kindest person I've ever known, and I'm so comfortable being around you. You mean a lot more to me than I thought. The highlight of every day is to come home and see your smile on video chat, even if only for a few minutes. That's why it would mean a lot to me if you would be my girlfriend?"

Aliyah never said a word, she just kissed me. For a long time.

"So that's a yes?" I asked.

"You're an idiot."

That night was a little different. I went home and texted her about the usual stuff, except it was different. She was my girlfriend. I went to school the next day happy. I honestly didn't care what anyone had to say to me. The next few months really started to fly. We went from spending a day or two over the weekend to seeing each other every afternoon. We went from making conversation to nothing but tongue and cheek. We slowly started to learn about each other. We learned our ins and outs. We became best friends.

For our six months anniversary, we decided to take a trip down the coast to a secluded cabin in the forest. As we pulled into the driveway, we finally both realized how secluded the cabin was. We were on a hill in the middle of a forest of trees four or five times taller than our roof, but they didn't obstruct the view of the ocean or the perfect views we witnessed.

As we pulled up in the driveway, I asked Aliyah if she was ready. She smiled back and opened her door. We grabbed our belongings and headed inside. The first room next to the door was the kitchen. It was small, but we planned on eating out, so it didn't matter. It flowed to the living room in an open plan arrangement. The walls were a deep blue, and it was a nice cute little cabin. To the right as you entered the living room was a hallway. There were two bedrooms down there along with a bathroom. We threw our bags in the bigger room and raced back to the living room. The balcony door was at the end of the living room and we found ourselves standing on the balcony in complete silence. I cuddled Aliyah from behind and kissed her on the neck. We didn't speak for a few minutes. We just stood there, embracing, in awe of the view.

"What are we going to do?" Aliyah asked, breaking the silence. "I'm thinking some fish and chips on the balcony, enjoy the sunset, and then some snacks with a good movie later."

It's not often I want to relax. I enjoy a good hike, eating out, and experiencing life, but it had been a long week, a long drive, and I was absolutely parched. Plus, enjoying life, the girl in front of me, her smile, the view, the sunset, it didn't get better than that.

We drove to get our fish and chips and our chocolate. The nearest town was a twenty-minute drive. We grabbed our food and headed back. At five-thirty in the evening, in September, so we caught the sunset perfectly. We sat ourselves on the floor of the balcony and began to eat.

"Thank you, babe," Aliyah started.

"Why?" I asked.

"For all this."

"You don't need to thank me."

"No, I'm serious. You didn't need to spoil me like this."

"This isn't spoiling you."

"I feel so special."

"It really isn't," I paused for a moment. "Besides why wouldn't I want to spoil the girl I love?"

Aliyah looked directly at me, her eyes lit up like the sky on new year's night.

"You love me?" she asked.

I slid over next to her. "I really do. I'm crazy about you. You're the first thing I think about when I wake up and the last thing on my mind before I fall asleep. I just can't help but think about our future together and when I'm going to see you next. I really do love you, Aliyah."

Aliyah never lost eye contact or let go of my hand. She just listened. "I love you, too, Brendan."

We finished watching the sunset before heading inside. We cuddled up on the couch, Aliyah laying on my chest.

She fell asleep about thirty minutes into the movie, so I

put the snacks in the fridge and carried Aliyah to bed.

We were awoken the next day by the sun gently warming our faces. It was nice and early, so we utilized the opportunity and decided to go for a hike through the bushlands and down along the beach. It was a calming experience right as the sun was rising. It was unreal how beautiful the light looked bouncing off the ocean. After our hike, we went for breakfast at a cafe in the town.

"How many kids do you want?" I asked.

"Kids, really?" Aliyah was stunned. It could have been that I asked out of the blue, or it could have been that we were teenagers, talking about kids after only six months together.

"You're asking about kids this early?"

"I was just curious. Don't tell me you haven't thought about it."

"I always liked the family I grew up in, so I'd prefer to have the same. Just a boy and a girl, with the boy being older."

"Yeah, I agree, I'd love the older boy to look after his little sister."

"Do you have any names?"

"I love the name Braith for a boy," I said.

"We're not naming our kid Braith. Where did you even get that name anyway?"

"The name came from Jesse. We used to love watching him play every time we could sit down and watch a game of American football."

"Braith, it rolls off the tongue so nicely, and I think I could get used to Braith." Aliyah stared at me and shook her head.

"I also love the name Sia."

"Really?" Aliyah asked. She was shocked. "One of my friends is named Sia. I can't wait for you to meet her, but I can't name my kids after her. It'd be too weird."

"But," I began, "it could be Aliyah and Sia, and I'll forever love it."

"It's definitely not happening now." Aliyah smiled as she said that.

Our waiter walked our meals over to our table. We both had the bacon and eggs, mine were scrambled and hers were poached. Just as she went to take her first bite, I asked, "What kid's names do you like?"

"I love Sydney, or even Indiana would be nice."

"Yeah, we could also call them Florida or Dakota or even California."

"Eewwww, no."

"That joke went straight over your head? Didn't it?"

"What joke?"

I winced a fair bit after that one and scratched the back of my head. "Geography isn't a strong point, either, is it?" I asked.

"No, why?"

"Florida, Dakota, and California are all states, just like Indiana. And well, Sydney is a capital."

"Oh . . . Right . . . Yeah, my friends have always given me grief because I thought Sydney was in Victoria."

I spat my water back into the cup.

"Stop it!" Aliyah demanded. "It's not funny!"

"Yeah, but come on, Sydney in Victoria?"

"Yeah, I know, it's wasn't my finest hour."

We finished our meals and headed home. It was a long drive but a fun one. This time Aliyah didn't fall asleep. She was the DJ. She chose some brilliant songs to sing along too but was always surprised I knew the lyrics.

I looked at her.

"It's my phone. Of course, I'm going to know the songs, you gaggle."

"You're an idiot. What's a gaggle?"

"Well," I began. "You aren't a regular goose. You're a flock of them. The whole flock. A gaggle of geese."

Aliyah was quiet. "You're a gaggle," she muttered.

Two months passed and I had finally graduated high school. I had decided to keep training for football and not go to university yet. In the mean time I was working any shifts available in the warehouses by the river front. It didn't bother me what I was doing as long as I came home to Aliyah every night. We fell more and more in love with every passing day. We saw each other every night, and I helped her study for her exams. Mid-November came around, and I received a phone call from an unknown number.

"Hello, is this Brendan, Brendan Thomas?"

"Yes, may I ask who is calling?"

"My name is Oliver, Oliver Higgins. We've been monitoring your football progress and wanted to invite you to come train with us."

"That'd be a pleasure, sir. Where?"

"That's the catch. I am involved at Southern Bombers."

"Like Western Australian Southern Bombers?"

"Correct."

"Like three thousand kilometers away Southern Bombers?" I questioned again.

"Yes."

"Oh." Stunned, I went dead silent.

"Look, we understand it's a huge move, but we would love for you to seriously consider as we believe we can help your ability. You'd be a great asset to our club."

"May I have some time to do some research and have a think?"

"Certainly, we will touch base with you next week if that's okay?"

"Sure! Enjoy your night."

"You, too," Oliver responded.

I had walked out of the room mid-conversation. I always felt rude talking on the phone around others. I walked back into the room to see Aliyah sitting on the bed, a very excited look on her face.

"Who is Oliver?" she asked.

"He's the coach of the Southern Bombers football club. He wants me to play there next year."

"That's so exciting, babe." Aliyah jumped off the bed and gave me a big kiss on the cheek. "Why aren't you excited?" She thumped my chest a few times. "Get excited!"

"Southern Bombers are in Perth."

"Like Western Australia Perth?" Aliyah asked.

I nodded.

"Like the other side of the country Perth?"

I nodded again.

Aliyah sat down on the bed in shock, the look of excitement replaced by one of sadness. "Well, what are you going to do?"

I sat down on the bed beside her and held her hand. "I don't know."

Aliyah stood up and faced me. "You have to go," By that stage, a tear had fallen down each of her cheeks. "It's your dream to play football. You have to go."

"It won't change my dream. They're a semi-professional club—kind of like a development league. I'll still train and wait for something closer to home." I stood up and grabbed both her hands.

"I'll always be right here. We can talk like the old days. Once I graduate, I can move over there. We can make this work," she said.

"I'm not going."

"Brendan, if you stay, I'll break up with you."

My eyes lit up in shock. "Why?" I asked.

"I'm not going to be the girl who ruined everything you worked hard for. I refuse to be that girl."

We both lay back down on the bed in complete silence. Aliyah nestled her head on my chest. We just lay there in shock, in sadness. Isn't it funny? Something you've always dreamed of having and worked incredibly hard for finally presents an opportunity, and you no longer want it. Sometimes the greatest opportunities come at the most inopportune times. Why couldn't a team in Victoria call me? Why couldn't I stay home? I made the call to Oliver the next morning, and I was on a four-hour plane ride back to Western Australia. I touched down on some very familiar surroundings. The sun was out. I hadn't seen that in a while. I was greeted by a very unfamiliar face. a tall, man, midforties, with brown eyes and brown hair, although it was starting to have streaks of grey running through it. He walked over to me in the terminal.

"Brendan Thomas?" he said with a questioning tone, yet a distinct presence to it.

I stuck my hand out to shake his.

"John Hume, club president," he said.

"Pleasure, sir," I responded.

"You must be tired. Let's get your bags and get you to your new home."

Mr. Hume carried my bags from the terminal to his car. We sat in his car and began the journey.

"Have you been told much about your living arrangement?" he asked.

"Nothing as of yet, sir."

"You can call me John. I don't mind."

"My dad raised me to address everyone by their last name or sir. I hope you don't mind. It's just habit."

"If that's what you're comfortable with, I can get used to

Mr. Hume." He paused and smiled. "I can get used to sir, too. Anyway, you will be living with me while you get on your feet. There are four of you coming across from Victoria. Jim, Ethan, and Hayden. You'll all be staying with me until then."

"Where are they all from?" I asked.

"Jim is from West Melbourne, Ethan is from Bendigo, and Hayden is from East Hawthorn. I don't have many rules other than be respectful, work hard, and clean up after yourselves."

I nodded. "Seems fair, sir."

"Oh, lastly, don't ever let me catch you eyeballing my daughters."

I laughed.

"No, I'm serious. One's your age."

"Is her name Chloe, sir?"

"Yeah, why?"

"I went to primary school with her."

"Bloody hell, when did you move to Victoria?"

"When I was eleven."

"Well, there you have it, small world."

We arrived at my new home. This house was truly something to aspire too. A ten-bedroom mansion on the canals, equipped with an indoor lap pool and a tennis court. The football club provided the bare essentials for living. I lived in a shared house with enough food and bills covered. Because it was semi-professional, they were able to do this through their sponsorship without paying a wage. This allowed the players to focus on training. But if you ever wanted extra you had to find a job of your own and manage your time effectively.

It was midnight, I went straight to bed and called Aliyah to let her know I was safe. We said our good nights, and I fell asleep. I was quite surprised over Aliyah staying up till three in the morning waiting for a phone call. It made me smile, but also made me realize how much I was going to miss her.

Next morning, I was woken up by knocking on the door.

"Hey, Brendan, you there?"

I didn't know who it was. The voice wasn't familiar, but it was a male.

"Brendan?" I heard again followed by a knock at the door.

"Yeah," I responded.

"Meet us downstairs in ten. We have early morning training."

I was tired, but none the less, it was time to begin. I sat up, put my hands on my face, and tried to comprehend what time it was. "Five am, you've got to be kidding me," I muttered under my breath as I walked downstairs to see the other three men sitting around the kitchen bench with Mr. Hume.

One of them stood up to shake my hand. "I'm Jim, Jim Cadel,"

"Brendan Thomas," I responded.

"Sorry for waking you up, mate. We have a big day ahead,"

Jim gestured to the man sitting on my right. He was a unit, six-feet-seven-inches tall with red hair. Easily one hundred and ten kilograms of pure muscle. He made me feel small.

"This is Ethan," Jim said. Ethan and I shook hands.

"Pleasure, mate," Ethan said.

"This is Hayden." Jim said, gesturing to Hayden.

Hayden shook my hand. "Pleased to meet you, buddy."

"What time did you come in?" Jim asked.

"I arrived just after midnight," I responded.

"Ahhh." They collectively sighed.

"Have you received your criteria for today?" Jim asked.

I laughed. "Not yet. I was hoping for a day to settle in."

"Noooooo," Hayden responded. "Straight into it, mate."

"Well, then no, I'm unaware of today's agenda."

Hayden turned to look at Mr. Hume.

"Johnny boy, one job, you had one job. You didn't even let him know what we're doing today?"

John scratched the back of his head. "Yeah, my bad. We were too busy sharing stories." He turned to face me. "Sorry, mate, you're in for a huge day."

Mr. Hume bought out a fair few pieces of paper, all stapled together, thick like a book. The first page had our pre-season schedule followed by a contract. Mr. Hume handed it to me.

"Everyone out the front in twenty-five."

I sat down and flicked through the criteria while I ate my breakfast. Today we were going to the club early to meet the coaching team and the team members that don't play.

We arrived at the club, where I received the official tour. There were a few people to meet along with the great facilities. They had just spent over two million on renovations, which meant all the equipment was new and professional. After the official tour, we headed to the beach to begin the training for the day. There were seventy men there. I was nervous but also quite excited over what the day would require from us. It was already thirty-two degrees at ten in the morning. There was not a cloud in the sky, and it was bloody hot.

Mad dog, the captain, welcomed me. "Rough morning to start, buddy. It's going to be a hot one."

He wasn't wrong. It was like the sand dunes added another ten degrees to the air. Mad Dog took me over to meet

Callo. He had won their Best and Fairest the previous two years. He also played at a professional level, but a torn ACL cut his career short.

"Callo, meet Brendan, Brendan, Callo," he said, gesturing toward me.

"Callo, Brendan is your shadow for the day," Mad dog said.

"Welcome, buddy." Callo put his arm around me and walked over to the starting point. "What's your biggest strength?" he asked.

We arrived at the starting point where the fitness trainer Marty was standing.

"I would have to say my aerobic capacity," I replied.

"That's a huge call, mate," Callo responded.

"What's a huge call?" Marty asked.

"Brendan here says his aerobic capacity is his biggest asset."

Marty looked me up and down and smiled. "It's a huge call indeed. Guess we will have to find out."

Training began, and I had never been through something so brutal in my life. Callo, Barbells and I led the pack by a fair margin. After about thirty minutes of hill sprints, Oliver the coach bought us in. Oliver was a smaller guy with a ripper mustachs. He must have been mid to late fifties. I can't say I knew much about him. I just knew when he spoke, no one moved.

"It's good to see you all working so hard. Just remember, today isn't about who is the fastest or the fittest. We have seventy blokes, and we want to know who won't give up. If you do, don't apologise to anyone. Just get in your car and better luck next year."

Oliver turned his back and walked off.

Mad dog spoke up. "That message was loud and clear boys. Now back to the bottom of that hill."

The day felt like forever. At midday, we were at the top of the dunes in forty degrees, sun shining down on us. I was hunched over next to Barbells, sweat pouring down from both of our faces.

"You gotta love it," Barbells said with a huge grin on his face.

I laughed before wiping the beads of sweat off my forehead with my forearm, which didn't seem to work as they were just as sweaty.

"Over here boys!" demanded Marty.

We walked over to see many different obstacles placed at the bottom of the dune.

"Ahh, shit," muttered Jim.

"What?" I asked.

"I've only been here a week, but I know trouble when I see it, and twenty-kilo kettlebells seem like a world of fun."

I hadn't even noticed. I was barely functioning, but my attention perked up when he said that.

"How are we all traveling?" asked Marty.

There was a collective group of murmurs under our breaths, which consisted of *good, fine,* and *all right.* Not one person sounded convincing though.

"I'm glad to hear that; You're all halfway through."

Marty paused. I think it was intentional to gauge our reactions. You've got to be a special trainer to put a team through that. You must have to get some sort of thrill from our pain.

Marty continued. "Now the fun stuff begins," he said, grinning.

I remember looking around at my then seventy teammates. Some were hunched over, hands on knees. Others were sitting on the ground, barely catching their breath. Some just had their hands in their hips. If there was ever a time to question what football was about, it was that exact moment right there, when you were defeated, when you had almost nothing left, but you kept trying for the mate beside you or the colors you had on your back. For everything those colors stood for, past, present, and future, that's what football was about.

Mad dog stood up. "Let's not waste any more time fellas. On ya feet."

As a collective, we stood up and walked over to the weights where we were joined by Coach Oliver. He stood there proudly, hand behind his lower back, feet shoulder-width apart.

"We're just messing with you guys." He smiled as he pulled out a gridiron ball. "Top effort today, guys. Go cool off in the water."

Oliver tossed Tyler the ball and all seventy men were full speed into the water, not even taking their training gear off.

Later that day we all caught a ride back to the club rooms in Mr. Hume's car.

"How was the first training session, rookie?" he asked.

"Insane, sir."

"Did you keep up?"

Ethan butted in. "The animal killed it."

All four of us looked at Ethan with a stunned look on our faces.

"The animal?" asked Mr. Hume.

"He's an animal, the kid's an endurance animal," Ethan responded.

Jim rubbed my head. "The animal, I love it."

I didn't say a word, but I loved it, too. It felt good to have a nickname but also to be accepted. When we got home, I hurried to my room and collapsed on my bed. I was completely knackered from training, and I wanted to lie down for five minutes before I got changed. We had to be at the club by four for dinner and drinks, to celebrate the start of another season.

It was a bloody long afternoon, but it was a brilliant opportunity to get to know some of the boys, along with some of the major figures around the club. It had come to eight, time to head home. I arrived at home, set up my laptop and asked Aliyah to jump online for our first video date. I waited for a while before I woke up the next morning to many missed phone calls and my laptop still open. As I was upset, I texted Aliyah to apologize, before heading downstairs to begin day two. This three-hour time difference was going to be annoying if all my days were going to be like that.

Time flew by in the process of finding a job and training every day. Aliyah would call me every night. It would be back to the way our relationship began, but every time I called her, I was never happy to see her. The distance never got any easier. I missed her a little more every time. The days did get easier, through being busy.

A quote I once heard became very true. "Missing someone isn't about how long you've been apart. It's about doing something and wishing they were there." It was true. The second I woke up, I missed her. My morning walk, I missed her. During work and training, she crossed my mind, but I was doing what I needed to do. The second I walked back in the door, I would instantly realise how empty the home seemed, and I missed her again. I just wanted to hear about her day and tell her about mine. I wanted to help make dinner and genuinely be silly. Instead, I was eating a microwaveable meal out of the fridge, laying down in an empty house. The worst part was when I logged onto video chat to see her beautiful smile, I was wishing it was right beside me. That's when I missed my best friend the most. Those reasons are why it was harder every time I logged on, yet it was the only way that made being on the other side of the world that much more bearable. The daily grind continued, and it was Christmas time, although I didn't have the money to fly home. Aliyah stayed up with me all night but eventually hit the hay. I can't imagine how much sleep she got, but I had plenty. By this stage, Ethan and Hayden had moved out together, Jim moved out with his girlfriend, and Mr. Hume had taken his family to Perth for the holiday season. I was all alone and besides a phone call home, there was nothing for me to do.

CHAPTER FIVE: HOME

It was February and I had been there for three months. It was late at night, and Aliyah was on a call with my family in the background.

"What do you want for your birthday?" she asked.

"Just a flight home," I replied.

Aliyah's emotions had abruptly shifted, you could see her grinning from ear to ear. It was a smile that I had not seen for quite some time.

"Can you get time off?"

"I suppose."

"When am I booking for? Actually, Wait."

The screen went completely black except for the message, *your chat session has now ended.* I immediately received a phone call from a very excited lady.

"I needed the laptop to book a flight," she told me. "When are you coming? How long for?"

I cut her off. "Calm down, calm down." I giggled, and she giggled.

"Okay," she continued, "when am I booking for?"

"I don't know, in two or three days," I replied.

"Okay three days away, and when do you have to go back? Can you get much time off three weeks away from footy season?"

"Maybe we could make it a one-way ticket, babe."

"What?" Aliyah replied,

"I said may —"

I was cut off by Aliyah. "I heard what you said. I meant

what? Why?"

"Because I miss you and I want to come home."

"Football is what you've always wanted to do."

"Yeah, I guess," I responded. She was right. "But my wants have changed."

I didn't hear even a whisper on the other end of the line. It was dead silent. For someone I thought would be so excited, I think she was just shocked.

"Well, it's booked. You leave Perth airport at six in the evening in two days."

Aliyah and I said our goodbyes before I rested my head on my pillow and closed my eyes. Although this time I was not upset, I felt like a little kid on Christmas. It was time to return home. I woke up the next day and went about my daily routines of my breakfast and morning walk, but I had a little strut in my step. I wanted to go home, so I was going through the motions as fast as I could. I went to training and admired every second. Every run, every kick, every high five. We completed our recovery before I went to speak to Oliver.

"What's up, Brendan?"

I shook Oliver's hand. "I'm going to head home, sir. I just wanted to thank you for the opportunity."

Oliver nodded before putting his other hand around mine. "It's been a pleasure having you. It's a big move for an eighteen-year-old. Maybe next year?" Oliver smiled.

"Yeah," I paused before answering and smiled back. "Maybe."

I walked out of there and said my final goodbyes before beginning my ride. It was a beautiful night, still thirty degrees but a nice cool breeze. I went straight to my room and began packing. There was no call tonight. I didn't have the time. I was seeing them all tomorrow. I walked downstairs the next morning to see Mr. Hume standing by the bench, eating his cereal.

"What's on the agenda today, Brendan?"

"I'm going to fly home."

"Is that right, huh?"

"Yes, sir," I responded.

Mr. Hume put down his cereal, walked over to me, and gave me a hug.

"Thank you for everything, I'm sorry I'm going," I told him.

"Don't ever apologize to anyone for seeking happiness. The heart wants what the heart wants."

I nodded.

"You'll write to me though?" he asked.

"Of course."

Mr. Hume placed both his hand on my shoulders. "I hope you know the door will always be open."

"Yes, sir."

"Then you take good care of yourself. It's been a pleasure."

"You, too, sir."

The rest of the day was a bit of a blur. It was me killing time, eagerly awaiting my flight. I jumped on the shuttle bus to Perth airport and began my trek home. Luckily my iPod had so many songs. It kept me occupied during my hour and half bus ride. I checked into my flight and found a nice bit of floor to cuddle up on. The final call came over the PA,

"Could all passengers traveling to Melbourne on flight 716, please head to gate twenty-seven. That's the final call for flight 716 to Melbourne, gate twenty-seven, please."

I picked up my gear and headed to the gate.

"You've been here since the first call, sir," the attendant said as I handed my boarding pass.

"Last on, last off, I like to avoid the congestion."

"Smart man," she said smiling. "But I reckon you're the only person in the last nine rows."

I was a bit taken away. "Are you joking? Why?" I asked.

"I think people don't want to sit near the bathrooms."

I was very happy. I could spread right out. "Guess I'll just be chilling with you guys then."

"Guess so," she responded.

She closed the gates as there were no other passengers in sight. We walked down the tunnel toward the plane.

"I'm Brendan by the way."

"Carly. Why are you heading to Melbourne?" she asked.

"It's time to go home," I replied.

I found my seat on the plane, and she was right. There were no other passengers for at least seven or eight rows. I was fine with it. It was time to relax and go home. I had never flown with this airline before, so I was intrigued to see what they were like. There were tv's in the headrest which was a very good start. I'm not sure if they were free or the channels were teaser channels to get you to buy the package, but the next few hours were going to be smooth, watching the Lakers take on the Knicks.

I touched down in Melbourne to see Aliyah, Dad, and Mum all waiting for me. My three-month long journey had come to an end, and I was glad to be home. I walked out of the gate to my Mum crying. She wrapped me up in her arms,

"I really hate that about you. Why are you always the last one off?" she asked.

"Hates a strong word," I said with a grin. I turned to Dad and gave him a kiss on the cheek.

"How was the flight?" he asked.

"Awesome, I watched Knicks and Lakers."

"Gridiron?" he asked.

"Nah, basketball."

"Who won?"

"Knicks by seven."

Dad nodded. "It's good to have you home."

"It's good to be home."

I turned to face Aliyah. She was a couple of meters away as she stayed back to let my parents say hello. She didn't say anything. She smiled straight at me. In my existence, I had never referred to Victoria as my home, not once, until I met Aliyah. That exact moment made me realise why. Home is where the heart is. In that exact moment, when she smiled, I realised what happiness was, that feeling that takes control of your body, that euphoria.

I had drawn out my words and put pauses in between them as I slowly made my way to her, step by step. "Sooooo . . . my . . . parents . . . get the . . .first . . .cuddle . . .because?" I put my hands around Aliyah's waist as she put her hands around my neck.

"I wanted your parents to love me," she replied.

"You're an idiot if you think they don't already."

Dad chimed in as he bumped me on the shoulder. "Come on, you two lovebirds. Let's go home."

We strolled on over to collect my baggage and began our car ride home.

"How was it?" Mum asked.

"How was what?" I asked.

"Western Australia? Playing football? Living out of home? The whole experience?"

"Umm, you know."

Aliyah hit me on the shoulder. "No, she doesn't. That's why she's asking."

I looked at Aliyah, then looked to Mum, who had turned around to face me from the front seat.

"Yeah, well it was so and so," I said jokingly, flinching to avoid Aliyah hitting me again.

"You're actually a shit head," Mum told me.

"What?" I responded. "I don't want to talk about me. I want to know how home was. I heard you got a coaching job, Dad?"

"Don't you try to change the subject," he added.

Mum wanted to hear the story, so I told her on the way home. We arrived home, and I wandered upstairs to put my clothes in my room.

"Are you staying the night?" I asked Aliyah.

"Am I allowed to?" she asked.

"Who cares?" I responded.

"I don't have any pajamas."

I reached into my suitcase to find my favorite jersey and favorite pair of footy shorts. Aliyah almost snatched them out of my hands with a big smile on her face. "I'm keeping these! Where do I get changed?"

I had resumed my work in the warehouses by the river, waiting for another opportunity closer to home. I had started playing with a local team. Although this time I was less optimistic. I knew opportunities were few and far between. But I was happy with my decision to come home. Year twelve was a tough year for Aliyah. She struggled a lot to keep up with all she wanted to accomplish. She was such a focused person. How someone can go to school, do four hours of dance, and then come home and continue to study into the night was beyond me. That's what she did. She wasn't willing to settle for second best, and the only real time we got together was when I was helping her with her homework. I was happy just to see her. I was happy to be a part of her life. It was lucky in the sense that she had five subjects and three of them I was great at, English, math, health and physical education. We got to spend a little bit of time together every night. I'll always believe that year twelve was perfect for our relationship. Leaving Western Australia was a tough decision. The heart wants what the heart wants. It wanted me to give up an opportunity of a lifetime, but as many late nights were had and many tears were shed, it was worth it. I came home to a smart, confident woman who I saw a bright future with. After spending three months apart, trying to help her study was totally fine with me. If anything, it made us stronger. We truly appreciated every moment together.

Aliyah's eighteenth birthday came around quite fast. I mean it was late September, the year was almost over. She came out of her room wearing a blue and white patterned jumpsuit. She looked breathtaking. We embraced each other before I put my arms around her waist.

"You look absolutely stunning."

She smiled. "Stop it." Aliyah continued, "Are you excited to meet all my friends?"

"I've met your friends, beautiful."

"You've met them in a passer-by way when we bump into them. Tonight, you're drinking and going clubbing with them."

"Of course, I'm excited. Are you excited to go out on the town for the time?"

"Only because you will be with me."

Aliyah's friends arrived one by one, greeting each other at the door. Before much time had passed, the girls were in their little group talking about this person and that in school, and I was sitting there with no involvement in the conversation, feeling like an outcast. That's always a problem with small parties. The people invited are very tight-knit. Mind you, only Maddy had a boyfriend, so I was short of options. All I had been hearing all week was, "I can't wait for you to meet Jeff. I hope you like him, I hope you really hit it off. I really want to double date with Maddy and Jeff."

. I was talking to Maddy with my back leaning against the

kitchen bench,

"When is he showing up? Why didn't you bring him?" I asked.

"He's coming with Sia. I don't know why they aren't here yet."

Sia was one of Aliyah's closest friends. They had danced together since they were four years old. Jeff was Sia's older brother, so it did make sense. Maddy received a message almost at that exact moment to come to the door. We both wanted to open the front door for them. I greeted Sia with a kiss on the cheek as did Maddy with Jeff.

"Jeff, this is Brendan," Maddy said, while signaling to me. "Brendan, this is Jeff."

Jeff and I shook hands.

"Nice to finally meet you, mate," I said.

"Yeah, you, too. These two have not shut up about this for quite some time. So much pressure."

"Oh, my God, you too? No offense, but I'm already sick of you. You wouldn't even believe it."

Jeff laughed. "Trust me, I would. I've been getting so many pep-talks, every day. "You have to like Brendan. We must double date,'" he said in a high-pitched voice.

I joined in. "If you two get along, you can play on the console while Maddy, Sia, and I hang out."

Sia hit Jeff on the arm, "Rude."

"Wait, you play?" Jeff asked.

"Yeah, why? Do you?" Jeff nodded.

"What games?" I asked.

"Basketball, gridiron, soccer, the sport-games really."

"Want to go play?" I asked.

"Definitely."

Jeff and I headed towards Aliyah's room before we heard Maddy follow us. "No. Where are you going? You have to meet my friends first!"

"But, but," Jeff responded.

Maddy crossed her arms and glared at him. "Five minutes, then you can play all night."

We wandered into the living room where everyone else was gathered. Jeff did the rounds, saying hello to everyone, while I continued to talk to Sia about how her family was and if school was treating her well. Jeff walked over to us.

"Did you have fun?" Sia asked.

"An absolute ball. They seem to know a lot about us," Jeff responded.

"Yeah, mate, how long have you and Maddy been dating?" I asked.

"Roughly, five months," Jeff replied.

"That's at least one hundred and fifty days and at least one hundred and fifty moments to talk about you and remind them all about you."

"I never looked at it that way."

There was a moment's silence between us all.

"So, uh, Sia, have you seen Aliyah's room?" I asked.

"No, why?" she answered. She had that look in her eyes, like I was an idiot, but in a joking way of course.

"Would you like to?" I asked. "It's pretty cool."

Sia looked at me dead straight in the eyes without breaking her gaze. "Brendan, not one part of me wants to see Aliyah's room. I'm sure it's exactly like every other room. I'm not going to play video games."

I put on my smart-ass voice like I was being very bitchy. "That's a shame, because it's pretty cool, and I would like to show someone."

Jeff sighed and rolled his eyes sarcastically. "Fine if you really want to show someone, I'll go with you."

I leaped up from the stool I was sitting on, and Jeff and I proceeded to head to the exit of the room.

Sia grabbed my arm. "Please don't leave me," she cried.

"LEL," replied Jeff.

"LEL?" I questioned.

"It's like LOL. It just rolls off the tongue better."

I nodded. "I like it."

"No serious guys, please don't leave me," Sia repeated.

I looked at Jeff, and we both looked back at Sia.

"Okay, bye!" we said in sync.

I didn't feel too bad. I knew her dance friends were only five minutes away, and if Aliyah saw her sitting by herself, she would go sit with her.

Jeff and I passed the kitchen on the way to grab another drink.

"What are we playing?" Jeff asked as he looked through the selection of games in the cupboard.

"Definitely basketball," he said as he grabbed the game out of the cupboard not giving me the chance to answer.

The game was a good one. I managed to pull off an overtime win over Jeff. We shook hands.

"Good game," he said before he paused. "But in no world does that team drop so many three-pointers, especially those deep ones."

I laughed. "I know, but I'm the king. I take sub-par players and make them relevant."

Jeff laughed uncontrollably. "The king, I love it." He kept laughing.

"You're correct, though. It does take some serious skill to make that team relevant, especially against a good team."

Maddy ran into the room, although she didn't make it into the room so to speak. She had her hands on both sides of the archway and leaned the top half of her body in the door.

"Do you two realise you been in here for over an hour?"

"Bullshit," I called.

"No, serious," Maddy replied.

Jeff pulled his phone out of his pocket to check the time.

"Wow, it's ten-thirty."

"Yes, it is," Maddy replied. She took a breath. "With ten-thirty comes speeches. Get your butts out here."

We both bounced up and hurried into the dining room where everyone had gathered. Trevor, Susan, and Aliyah were at one end while everyone else had gathered around them. There was a surprising amount of people there for only close friends. I guess, once you included her group from school, her group from dancing, and family, the numbers added up quickly.

Aliyah wrapped her arms around my waist when I reached them, and Trevor began to speak.

"Excuse m-me ev-eryone, I'm not great at speeches b-b . . . ut I'll give it my best effort." He paused for a moment and looked down at the piece of paper he was holding. His hands were shaking. "I remember this little girl since obviously the first day I met her." Everyone smirked. Trevor wiped his forehead with his forearm. Aliyah put her arms around Trevor's waist as he rested his arm on her shoulder. "You've grown up so fast, and I'm so proud of the beautiful woman you are becoming. I just hope I can always be around as hopefully . . ." Trevor paused. Everyone was intrigued with where he was going. " . . . hopefully wherever you go in life, I will always be in the running for number one. I may not win, but I hope you can at least consider me."

Aliyah smiled. "You'll always be number one, Dad."

"Ha ha, nice try, sweetheart, but you're growing up and going out your first time." Trevor hit me on the arm. "Take care of my princess tonight," he said jokingly but with a stern voice. "Honestly, I'm glad to be a part of your life, and I look forward to whatever the next chapter brings. Everyone, please raise a glass to toast Aliyah."

Everyone raised their drinks and took a drink. "You're up, big fella," Trevor said while staring at me.

I took a step forward and turned back to Aliyah.

Jeff raised his beer. "Woo, speech, yeah."

Everyone giggled.

"For those of you who don't know me, I am Brendan, the boyfriend. I don't want to say too much, but rather thank you for being here tonight and many more who would have if you didn't try to keep this small." I turned to face Aliyah. "Really good job, by the way." There were a few chuckles from the crowd. "I just want to thank you on behalf of everyone for putting smiles on our faces." I was nervously playing with my hands at that stage. "You make a lot of peoples' days, especially mine. You'll never understand how much I truly appreciate you."

Aliyah smiled as she walked over to give me a hug.

Jeff yelled from the back. "You big cutie."

There were some giggles, but I never broke eye contact with Aliyah. We both smiled and looked around the room.

"I ask everyone to raise a glass. You have brought something special to everyone in this room, and for that we are going to show you the greatest night of your life. To Aliyah."

Everyone joined in. "To Aliyah."

For the rest of the night, there wasn't much else to say. It went how every eighteenth should. We played some beer pong before heading out for a night out on the town. One of the girls from dance, Lauren, was a promoter for where we decided to go. We got the VIP treatment, which included no wait in line, a private booth, and our first round of drinks for free. It wasn't like any of the times I'd been clubbing. We just sat there drinking and talking. That's all there was. Not much dancing, just six of her closest friends, Jeff and me. That's another reason why I always knew how incredible she was. She was relaxed, down to Earth, and wanted to be around those who meant the most to her.

It didn't feel a long time before I was seeing her friends again. It was the end of the year and time for graduation. Aliyah had been stressed to say the least, but I admired her dedication and wanting to achieve the highest grade she could. Seeing her in her long flowing, elegant, black dress, her make-up done right up, and her hair professionally done for probably the first time in her life, I felt nothing but pride. She looked so beautiful and especially in black. We all met at Aliyah's and caught the limousine to the girl's school. There were some spots around the college to get some photos of the girls with their partners. We then left for the hall where all the parents were waiting. I walked in holding her hand.

"Are you nervous?" I whispered in her ear.

"Why would I be?" she responded.

"I know you don't like being around big audiences let alone getting on stage in front of them."

"Yeah, I suppose, but this time is different."

"Why?" I asked.

"Because I have you."

Aliyah leaned over and kissed me on the cheek. Nothing compares to the feeling of being appreciated by somebody you truly idolize. Aliyah enjoyed the whole night with her closest friends while I admired from afar. Jeff had plenty of mates there, so I met a few new people. The night ended with the girls getting ready to go to town. I chose to stay at home and let them enjoy a girl's night.

Aliyah came over and kissed me.

"It's time to go home," she said.

"Aren't you going out?"

"Yeah but I really don't feel like it." Aliyah put her hands around my neck. "I want to spend my time with you."

I took her hands off my neck and kissed her. "Go with your friends. They're leaving."

"Can I please?" she asked.

"Don't ever ask permission to hang out with your friends, especially on a night like this. Besides we have plenty of other days to spend time together."

I was awoken by a phone call from Aliyah at four in the morning.

"Can you pick me up?" she asked.

"I'll see you in five. Do we need to take anyone home?" I asked.

"Just Ellen if that's okay?"

"Of course."

We were lying in bed, facing each other. "How was your night?" I asked.

"A bit of fun. God, the town is full of sleazy men. Like what part of what guys do, do guys think is attractive?"

I looked at Aliyah very confused. "You'll have to try that one again, babe."

"What?" she asked.

"Explain what you meant. It made no sense."

"Oh," Aliyah laughed. "That explains your face. Just like guys are hell sleazy, they won't ever talk to you or sit around in the booth. They never introduce themselves, but when you get up to dance, they come from everywhere and try to dirty dance on you. All the girls just wanted a night out with each other."

"It's shit, isn't it?" I didn't really mean to smile, but it was nice to know the whole group loved each other's company and never craved the attention of guys.

"Yeah, I've got one of the good ones." Aliyah said as she grabbed my spare hand. "One that can hold a conversation, one who cares and just wants to make people happy."

"Stop with the compliments." I shook my head, but I could never stop smiling. The reason why I loved her was the little things like that.

"Anyway, you should probably get some sleep. You've got to be up early tomorrow."

"Why?" Aliyah asked. "I was planning on sleeping in tomorrow."

"That's a shame," I muttered. "Ahh, well, I guess you will have to sleep on the plane."

"Stop it!" Aliyah stated.

"Stop what?" I questioned.

"Pulling my leg. We aren't going anywhere."

"Oh, aren't we?"

"Where are we going?"

"Nowhere, apparently."

"Oi, serious, where are we going?"

"You said nowhere."

Aliyah punched me in the arm. "Tell me!"

I winced in pain and rolled over to face the wall. "That really hurt!" I exclaimed.

"Stop being a gaggle. Where are we going?"

"We are going to Sydney for a few days as a graduation present," I stated.

Aliyah looked at me in shock. "Are you actually serious?" I smiled and nodded. "We leave tomorrow?" she asked. I nodded again. "What time?"

"Our flight is at the airport at three, so leave here at one-thirty?"

Aliyah wrapped me up in her arms. "Thank you so much!" She bounced up, out of bed and ran to her wardrobe. "You gave me no time to pack! I have to pack!" She began to settle into a form of panic. "You can do this to a girl, Brendan! A girl has so many outfits to choose from!"

I picked Aliyah up and carried her back to bed, laid her down, and tucked her in. I kissed her on the forehead. "No need to panic now, beautiful. We can do it in the morning. Right now, you need to get some rest. Have the sweetest dreams, Aliyah."

Aliyah nodded off almost immediately, and I did, not too long after.

I was awakened abruptly the next morning by somebody shaking me. I opened my eyes slightly to see Aliyah staring at me. She tapped me lightly on the face.

"Best friend! Why are you sleeping?" she asked. I giggled. Aliyah bounced straight out of bed. "Best friend! We have to pack!"

I could hear the sheer excitement in her voice, something I hadn't heard for quite some time. She could never do anything half-heartedly, so juggling all she did over the past year meant her sleep had been sacrificed, especially for the last three months. That's why I was thrilled to see her the way she was about our little holiday.

"I'm just going to nap a bit longer," I said. I lay back down and closed my eyes, I was abruptly hit in the face by a pillow.

"You can sleep on the plane. Get up!"

You could hear the excitement grow more and more in her. She was on the move. I felt a tug on my right leg. She was literally trying to drag me out of bed.

"Best friend, let's go!" I bought my hands my face and rubbed my eyes. I stared straight at Aliyah. "It's eleven o'clock, and I'm a boy. I don't need to pack yet. I've got two and a half hours."

We touched down in Sydney and took the hour-long cab ride to our hotel. It was an awesome idea. The cab driver was an Aussie bloke who told us all the little things to do and places to eat. We checked in at the hotel and took a nap. I've never been able to sleep on planes, and I needed some rest. It was perfect timing. We skipped most of the heat and wandered out of our room around seven o'clock for a beautiful first evening. We were staying just off the main Street, right in the heart of Sydney. We followed main Street with the bridge in sight, before stopping to eat some dinner at a French restaurant located at the top of a fascinatingly designed building, probably every architect's dream to design something so off-key. After finishing dinner, we continued down main Street through all the buildings and finally made it to the bridge. I know they're just a bridge and a building, but the Harbour Bridge and the Opera House at night was truly a mesmerizing experience.

Moments like those always are better when it's with the company you have. We both didn't say much the whole time we were there. We were in awe of the experience. We spent almost two hours walking around the Quay. It was a cloudless night, and although there was a little wind, it was perfect in our coats. We walked slowly, hand-in-hand. I glanced over at Aliyah, grinning from ear to ear like an idiot.

"What?" she asked. I didn't answer her. "What?" She was a bit firmer this time. I still didn't respond. "No seriously, tell me!" she demanded.

"You're just . . . you're just the most beautiful person in the whole wide world."

She was the one grinning from ear to ear and smiling like an idiot. Although she kept her head toward the ground and slightly turned away from me to try and mask her smile. "Stop it!" she said faintly.

We stopped walking, I turned to face her, our hands joined near our waists.

"No, I'm serious," I told her. "I really appreciate you. You will never understand, but I'm glad I have you. This holiday wouldn't be the same. It's the company that makes it awesome."

Aliyah kissed me, "I appreciate you more. You don't

understand."

We kept walking, hand-in-hand, slower than before. Where we came from isn't a big city. I never realized how romantic a city's night lights can be. We arrived back at the hotel and snuggled up in bed to watch a movie and awoke to sunshine at six in the morning. I've always been a fan of natural light flooding in through the window to wake me. We decided to get up and go for a morning walk.

"Where are we walking today?" Aliyah asked.

"I'm thinking we start at Darling Harbour and go from there."

We began our hike for our first morning in Sydney. It was twenty degrees, sunshine, and no clouds. Darling Harbour couldn't have been more picturesque.

"You've graduated now. How's my big girl?" I asked.

"It feels so weird. Although it hasn't hit me properly, yet, because we always get holidays."

"Yeah, I suppose, it may take a few months. What are you going to do?"

"I'll see what offers I get. I've applied for teaching at the university."

"You would be good at that."

"Yeah, I guess, but I don't really know. Maybe I could be a nutritionist or something." Aliyah seemed to be getting lost in her own thoughts. "I would love to do clothing and styling for TV shows. I love doing that. That's what I would want to do most."

"Then do it," I responded.

Aliyah glanced at me weirdly. "Do you how hard it is to get into that business? There are limited spots, and you have to be really good."

"So what?" I asked. I never gave her the chance to respond. "You have the ability to be brilliant at anything you put your mind to. I reckon you should go for it."

There was a moment of silence. I think we both didn't know what to say. I broke the quiet.

"Let's look at it this way," I said. "What would be the steps in becoming behind-the-scenes prep girl?"

"That's what you're calling it?" Aliyah's asked.

I answered the question with another one. "What would you call it?"

Aliyah looked at me with a questioning glare. "Yeah, good call, I guess. Maybe a stylist?"

"So?" I asked her, "Why don't you get some sort of personal assistant role?"

"Because that's different. I don't really want to make coffee. I more want to prepare and style people."

"I know, but wouldn't you still learn along the way? Wouldn't people teach you everyone they knew as you worked?"

"Yeah, I suppose."

I could tell Aliyah was of two minds about it all.

"You've got plenty of time to decide. I think you would ace all three, but it wouldn't hurt to look for a traineeship of some sort and maybe defer university for a while to decide if you like it or not."

"I actually might. I like that idea."

Aliyah burst out laughing. She tapped me on the shoulder and pointed off into the distance to a lady walking much like we were, except she was wearing incredibly short shorts, and barely a sports bra. When she walked, she swung her arms over her head and back down. I couldn't help but laugh, also. I'm not one to judge people getting outdoors and doing exercise, but surely, she was aware of what was going on.

We were at the end of Darling Harbour taking in all the view had to offer. Some people live in houses you couldn't even dream about. We followed the trail around Walsh Bay and passed under the bridge. The bridge was a nighttime attraction, or I'm a night time person. It was not half as lovely in the daytime without the glow of the lights. We continued around the quay before making our way through the heart of the city, only stopping at random venues along the way.

In the middle of the day, the middle of summer was way too warm. We took comfort in the air-conditioned hotel room, trying to save some energy to experience the evening. We ended up sleeping until four when I woke Aliyah.

"Hey, sleepyhead!" I said as I lightly shook her, till she woke.

Aliyah rubbed her eyes. "What time is it?"

"It's four," I responded.

"How long have I been asleep?"

"I'm not sure, I think it's been three or so hours."

Aliyah looked at her watch. "I'm so sorry."

I smiled, she always cared about the small things like leaving me alone while she napped.

"What are we going to do?" I asked her. I had a few ideas but wanted to know if Aliyah really wanted to do anything.

"I'm not too sure," she responded. "What can we do?"

"I'd love to go have a look around at the shopping malls and maybe grab some dinner."

Aliyah stared at me. "Really? That's what you really want to do? You want to go shopping?"

I smiled and nodded, "I don't get to go out in the city much. I love getting lost in the buildings."

"Well, okay then." Aliyah burst out of bed and was ready to go.

We began our trek back into Sydney. We walked everywhere. We loved being active and having the opportunity to talk to one another. We arrived in the center of Sydney and immediately were lost. Aliyah was like a little kid in a candy store. Five stories high, her favorite store was five stories. After a couple of hours in there, she decided she needed another day tomorrow to complete the store. We wandered across the road to continue our shopping. There were so many stores and four hours had passed. We called it a night, grabbed some dinner and made our way back. We snuggled up in bed. Aliyah was playing with my hands before she lifted her head off my chest to face me. "Thank you for today."

"Don't you ever thank me for that again."

"No, I really don't think you realize how much I appreciate it. It wouldn't have been the greatest day for you."

I kissed Aliyah the forehead, "I appreciate you. I enjoy exploring, spending time with you, and seeing you smile. Today was a perfect day for me, too." Aliyah smiled. "Now go to sleep, beautiful. We have another huge day of exploring ahead of us before we have to go home."

"What are we going to do? Aliyah asked.

"I was thinking a walk through the Botanical Gardens in the morning, followed by breakfast or lunch with some shopping."

"No!" Aliyah responded. "Let's do something else. There's got to be plenty to do in Sydney."

"You haven't bought anything yet. It's your graduation present. You haven't even got any mementos to take home."

"But–but."

"No buts about it, Aliyah. We've seen the basics. It's been awesome. Now let's do some serious shopping. If we miss anything, I'm sure we can pop up for the weekend at a later date."

We woke up the next morning and put on our walking gear. We started down one of the main streets when we came across an Anzac Memorial Park. We stopped in the memorial park to pay respects. I've never been to other countries, but the legend of the Anzacs was something every Australian was proud of. Every Australian I knew wanted to pay their respects to the brave men and women who made the ultimate sacrifice for our country. That was why we stopped. We were there for well over an hour, and the place was packed.

We continued to walk and talk all the way through the Botanical Gardens. I didn't realise how much you can appreciate flowers until you enter the gardens. It's so calming and serene. We eventually made it back to the hotel and packed our belongings before heading off to begin our last day of shopping.

Once in the elevator, Aliyah moved her right arm around like a windmill while placing her left arm on her shoulder, she seemed to be wincing.

"Are you okay?" I questioned.

She tried moving her neck. "Yeah, I think I'm sunburnt."

"Sorry. Our walk went a little longer than planned."

"No, it was awesome!"

We looked at each other.

"At least we get to spend the rest of the day indoors and in air-conditioned shops," I said.

"I suppose," Aliyah mumbled, stepping out of the elevator. "Can we get lunch first?"

"What do you want?" Aliyah cheekily grinned. "What?" I asked. She just kept grinning. "Tell me what you want!"

Aliyah raised her voice. "It's not that easy!"

We both laughed, and people looked at us weirdly. I'm assuming they didn't realize we were quoting the *Notebook*.

"Seriously, what do you want for lunch?" I asked.

Aliyah looked at the ground. She shyly said, "You won't be happy."

I was puzzled at this stage, I didn't know what to say. "What is it?" I asked.

Aliyah pointed up ahead, about two-hundred meters in the distance. "Can we have chicken and chips?"

I laughed. "Yeah, definitely."

We had a feast before walking further down the street to continue our shopping from the previous day. After a few hours of being dragged around to shop after shop came the best part, storing everything Aliyah bought in our suitcases. That was a task. Our gear was spread everywhere. I was standing up with my hands on my hips, scratching the back of my head.

"Yeah, look, we're going to need another suitcase," I told her.

Aliyah smirked, "My bad."

I laughed, "I knew you bought a lot, but good job lying to me."

"I honestly thought I had more room in my suitcase, I swear!" she exclaimed.

"Stress-less, we will just have to make it fit."

She seemed upset, asking, "Are you angry with me?"

I wrapped her up in my arms before taking a step back and putting my hands on her shoulders, I looked straight into her eyes. "Not even in the slightest. I'm actually quite impressed."

"You're lying," she claimed.

"Nah, serious, mate."

We somehow manage to squeeze every bit of clothing in-to my bag and began our journey home. It was a long one, with peak hour Sydney traffic to the airport, and then our plane was delayed by four hours. We just hung out by the boarding gate. An announcement came over the PA, "Now boarding flight 3172 to Melbourne, gate seventeen. Flight 3172 to Melbourne, gate seventeen."

A massive sigh came over the whole room. It could've been a sigh of relief, or it could've been that we had to move down the terminal to a different boarding gate to join a long line that moved very slowly. We handed the lady our boarding passes.

"That suitcase looks a bit big for carry-on," she said.

"You guys allowed me to have this on the way up," I responded.

"They shouldn't have. Can you please pop it in a measuring basket?"

The lady gestured to her left to a steel casing of the maximum requirements. I walked over. It didn't fit in. "What happens now?" I asked.

"We have to not allow the suitcase on the flight."

I looked her at her little frustrated. "Look, lady, I don't mean to be rude, but I've just waited five hours. At any stage, I could have checked this in as proper luggage and not carry on, but they allowed it on the way up, so I didn't think I needed to. Now I'm roughly five meters away from getting on the flight, and you're going to tell me it's not allowed? I just want to go home."

"I could call the luggage loaders to see if they can check it in that way, but there will be a fee."

"That would be lovely," I replied.

The hostess made a call to baggage. "Yeah, yeah, okay." She put down the phone.

"They will take a bag for thirty dollars."

I handed it over. "Thank you."

Aliyah and I walked down the bridge to the plane.

"I'm really sorry," Aliyah said sheepishly.

"Why?" I asked.

"For making the suitcase too big."

I smiled. "Don't be sorry, beautiful. It was too long anyway. It was just frustrating that they allowed it on the first time. I would have happily checked it in five hours ago if I knew. Besides who cares anyway?"

We walked on the plane and took our seats.

"You better wear the shit out of those clothes now, though."

Aliyah smiled. "I intend to."

CHAPTER SIX: JINGLE BELLS

"Wake up! wake up!" Aliyah shook me hard, "Wake up! It's Christmas!" She was jumping for joy and bouncing on the bed. The excitement was contagious.

I wrapped her up in my arms. "Merry Christmas, beautiful."

"It's our first Christmas, you handsome man! What are we going to do?"

"I think we should go jump on everybody else." I didn't even get to finish my sentence before Aliyah leaped out of bed. She grabbed my arm and tried to pull me with her.

"Let's go wake everyone. We have so many presents to unwrap."

We walked into Trevor and Susan's room and jumped on the bed.

"Rise and shine. It's present time," Aliyah yelled.

"Oh, my God," cried Susan. They both couldn't even open their eyes. "What's the time?" Susan asked.

"Just after seven," I responded.

Trevor and Susan both looked very stagnant with no intention of waking or moving.

"What time were you guys up to?" I asked Trevor.

"I think we got to bed after four. That's when we finished wrapping the gifts."

I felt so bad. They were struggling to function. I struggled to function on six hours sleep, let alone only three.

"All the more reason for you to want to wake up and give them to us!" exclaimed Aliyah.

Aliyah wasn't spoilt. She just loved Christmas and would happily over-excite herself in hopes of bringing everyone to her level.

"We will go make you a coffee."

Aliyah ran out the room to boil the kettle before coming back to grab me.

"Mark and Hannah?" I asked. She nodded all seriously.

We burst the door open to see Mark with his finger out. "Don't you dare jump on the bed," he warned.

"Aww!" cried Aliyah. "Have you guys been up long?" she asked.

"I set my alarm for seven, so you wouldn't come jump on us."

"How'd you figure seven?" Aliyah questioned.

"Mum and Dad would never ever let us get up before then. I figured we would keep the tradition."

"Fair point." Aliyah added, "But get out of bed because it's time to open presents. Santa's been here!"

Aliyah proceeded to turn around and walked out of the room before looking back over her shoulder at Mark and Hannah. "Oh, and one last thing." She ran over and leap-frogged onto the bed before getting up and walking out. "That's all," she said as she exited the room.

We all gathered at the entrance.

"Now that you've woken all of us up, are you able to go grab your brother?" Susan asked Aliyah.

"I'll call him." Aliyah went off to find her phone as we all gathered in the living room near the tree.

"Jesus, there's a lot of presents here," I said.

"Yeah, look, I'm not surprised you guys were up so late," Mark had said that just as Aliyah walked in the room.

"What's the verdict?" he asked.

"Andy said to give him ten minutes to wake up and have

a ciggy."

We all stared.

"His words, not mine. He also said Linda will be over after lunch so we can open presents this morning." Aliyah added.

I stood up. "Anyone want a tea?" I asked.

"Another coffee would be brilliant," Susan responded.

"Sure, anyone else?" No one responded.

I made my way to the kitchen with Aliyah. We did a quick tidy up before the kettle boiled and took a seat back on the couch as Andy walked in.

"Bout time!" Mark exclaimed.

"It's seven-thirty. Chill or you're not getting your present."

Mark acknowledged Andy. "That's still a serious improvement on the present I got you."

Andy stared straight at Mark. "You better be bloody joking, mate!"

"Payback is a bitch!"

We all laughed, but Andy didn't seem too thrilled at the idea.

"Whatever," he said. "Let's just get this done."

Handing out the presents, Trevor played Santa, as I'm sure most dads do. We finished unwrapping all the presents. When we got to the final one, Trevor picked it up. "To Andy, from Mark, P.S. suck it!" Trevor handed the present to Andy.

"I'm not opening it," he said.

"Just open the present. I need to get back to Bed," Susan ordered.

"No, it's not happening!" Andy stated.

Mark sang to him. "You're going to hate it. You're going to hate it."

"Shut up!" demanded Andy. "It isn't funny!"

"Only to you," Trevor said as he was in hysterics. "Just open it, mate."

Andy unwrapped the big box. It was empty.

He threw the box on the ground, "I'm going to have a ciggy. Merry Christmas. I'll see you all at dinner."

As Andy slammed the door behind him, Mark walked over and picked up the partially unwrapped present and turned back the top flap of the box. "I guess I'll be going to the Comedy Festival opening night then." We all kept laughing. "It's probably one of the best presents I've ever bought him," Mark said as he placed the tickets with Andy's other presents.

"Well," Susan and Trevor stood up. "We're going to get some rest so we can whip you all up a nice lunch and dinner."

Aliyah and I gave everyone a quick kiss and cuddle before retreating to our bedroom.

"Have you got much to pack?" I asked.

"No, I'm ready, are you?"

"I'll grab my keys," I said.

As we left the house Aliyah shouted, "Merry Christmas everyone!" She shut the front door behind us. As we arrived at my parents' house, Aliyah opened the door. "Merry Christmas!" she shouted again. My sister ran downstairs and greeted us with a smile from ear to ear.

"Bout time you two got here!" She hugged us both. "How have you been, little bro?"

"The usuals. How's work?" I asked.

"The usuals." Theresea grabbed Aliyah's hand, "How dare you take my little brother away from me! Who am I supposed to open Santa sacks with at four am?"

Aliyah shrugged.

Theresea led Aliyah upstairs by her arm. "Come on, Brendan. There's so much to show you." The three of us ran upstairs, passing Theresea's room. She opened the door, grabbed a piece of clothing, and threw it at her boyfriend, Steve. "Get up, you lazy shit. It's Christmas!" She grabbed her Santa sack and shouted, "Love you!" as she closed the door. We ran down to my room,

"Santa bought you so much cool stuff!" Theresea added.

"You looked through his Santa sack?" asked Aliyah.

"Yeah! He takes way too long to wake up normally." Theresea replied. "Anyway, open it!"

I handed my Santa sack to Aliyah. "You do the honors?"

Aliyah started fishing through, pulling all sorts of presents out. "Babe," she said with her hand in the sack. "That's a lot of chocolate."

"That's just breakfast, babe," I replied.

Aliyah dug into the sack to find doubles of all the chocolate along with an envelope. She opened it and began to read aloud. "Dear Aliyah, I wasn't sure what address you would be at, have a Merry Christmas, regards Santa."

"What did he leave?" I asked.

"How nice of Santa," Theresea added.

Aliyah opened the card to see two tickets to the ballet. She covered her mouth with her left hand.

"How did the elves even make that? That's bullshit." I said jokingly.

Aliyah was shocked but appreciative none the less.

"That's all that's in there. What did you get, Theresea?"

Theresea's eyes lit up. "I got the same as you guys with the chocolate, but most importantly, I get to sleep with my boyfriends."

"You put an S on that." Aliyah pointed out.

"I'm aware of that," Theresea said with a grin from ear to ear.

Aliyah and I looked at each other, curious to what she meant.

Theresea paused as she reached into the Santa sack. She pulled out tickets to her favorite boyband along with a quilt cover.

Aliyah and I collectively sighed. "Oh, well, that makes sense," I said.

"Have you washed them yet? So, you can put them on your bed?" Aliyah asked.

Theresea shook her head.

"Let's go do what we all do best and wake everybody up for breakfast, so you can wash your cover," said Aliyah.

"Deal!" Theresea ran in to get Steve up while Aliyah and I ran into Mum and Dad's room. Aliyah jumped on the bed while I played with Daffy, our Labrador.

"Merry Christmas!" she yelled, as she leaped from what looked like five meters away.

We woke the whole family and went downstairs for our first Christmas breakfast together. I had always watched my brother and sister smile with their partners, wishing I had that. The whole breakfast I saw the side of Aliyah I had never seen, a side that left me smiling constantly for the whole time. She was witty and sassy every time to Dad when he tried to be a smartass. She had a few good conversations with Mum while she helped cook. She was comfortable. She was perfect. After missing Christmas last year, the stresses of her final year of school, and not really being able to see each other frequently, to see her clicking with my family was the best present I could ever have asked for.

We unwrapped all the presents and started the journey back to Aliyah's house for dinner with her parents. We were driving, and I was holding Aliyah's hand. She turned and looked at me, "What are you smiling at?" she asked.

"I'm just grateful," I replied.

"For what?"

"You."

I didn't turn to look at Aliyah. There was nothing but silence after that. I only felt her grip of my hand tighten.

After a few moments passed Aliyah spoke. "I really love you, Brendan."

"I will always love you more, I promise."

"No, you don't! I truly appreciate you for who you are and everything you've done for me."

I tightened my grip on Aliyah's hand. "I'm just so glad we found each other."

We arrived at Aliyah's house and walked in the front door. It was silence — everyone must've been at their partners' houses.

"Do we wake up Mum and Dad?" Aliyah asked.

"I think we should let them rest. Maybe we could cuddle up and watch a movie?"

"I'd love that."

We laid down in bed Aliyah snuggled up on my chest. "Hey, beautiful," I said.

"Yeah?"

"Merry Christmas." I gave her a kiss on the forehead and handed her my carefully wrapped present. She leaned down beside the bed to grab present she had wrapped for me.

"Open it," she said as she handed it to me.

"Nah, no fair. I handed you yours first."

Aliyah unwrapped her present. She pulled the bracelet out and put it on her wrist.

"It has a locked heart with a key. I love it!" she exclaimed.

She then pulled out a necklace. It was just a plain chain with the centerpiece. She read the centerpiece quietly. "True-love is eternal." Aliyah proceeded to put both pieces of jewelry on.

"Did Brendan do okay?" I asked.

Aliyah kissed me on the lips. "Brendan did excellently. Now open yours."

I wasted no time, Aliyah kept bragging that I was going to love it, so I was excited.

"No way!" It was tickets to my favorite comedian, and she was right, I loved them.

We lay back down and finish watching the movie before it was time to help with dinner preparations. Aliyah helped her Mum with the cooking while I helped her Dad tidy and set up the house for visitors. A feast with people we hadn't seen in a while followed. It's always nice to see family you don't get to opportunity to see during the year, but we didn't stay long. We'd agreed to spend the night at my parents since we woke up at Aliyah's.

We made the drive back out there and greeted Mum and Dad. They had already had a few celebratory drinks with my brother and sister, so we wasted no time in joining them. We started drinking and playing a few board games before a few had to retire due to work on Boxing Day. I was left with my brother, my father, and Aliyah.

"What are we going to do?" Dad asked.

"Have you ever played King's Cup?" I asked.

Dad shook his head.

Aliyah, Ben, and I looked at each other before Aliyah looked back at Dad.

"You're in for a real treat," she said as I went to the cupboard and found a bowl big enough.

Ben and Aliyah explained the rules.

"Let's do this." Dad was excited for his first time to play.

Ben drew a king on the first card and poured his whole drink into the bowl before going to the fridge to grab another. I was next. I drew a nine.

"Time to rhyme, I guess," I said.

"Wait, wait," said Dad. "What do we do?"

"Brendan will say a word, and you must rhyme with that word. If you can't think of a word or if you repeat someone else's word, you lose and must drink. Understand?" Aliyah asked.

"Got it," Dad replied.

"Ready?" I asked Dad.

"Yeah, but don't make it too hard."

"I won't." I paused for a second, just to help with the suspense. I looked Aliyah directly in the eyes. "The word is orange."

Dad and Ben laughed at me.

"You're an asshole," Aliyah said as she took a drink. "My turn now."

"What are you even going to do?" Dad asked her. "You just got rolled."

Aliyah tried to ignore the comment. Aliyah smiled as she looked at the card she drew.

"It's a jack." She showed the jack to all of us.

"What's a jack?" asked Dad.

"Rule maker," I sighed as I told him she got to make any new rule she wanted to, expecting to get hit hard.

Dad sighed once I told him, too.

"What are you going with?" Ben asked.

Aliyah thought, but only for a moment.

"Every time Bill drinks, he has to drink double."

"Oh, wow," I said.

"Jesus," Ben chimed in with.

Dad never said a word. He sat there glaring at Aliyah. Aliyah just laughed. "Guess you got rolled, Bill!"

"Is that so?" he asked. Aliyah just kept laughing.

"I will remember that." Dad looked around. "Is it my turn now?"

"I believe so," said Ben.

Dad reached in to grab a card, muttering to himself. "Please be a jack, please be a jack." He kept the card close to his chest.

"What'd you get?" we all asked simultaneously.

Dad showed us, sounding excited. "I got an eight!"

"Snap!" I said.

"That sucks so bad," Ben said, and Aliyah couldn't hide her laughter.

"Wait, what's an eight?" asked Dad.

"Finish your drink," Ben told him.

"I only just poured this one."

"Doesn't matter," I said.

Dad looked devastated. "It's straight scotch."

"Doesn't matter," I repeated. "They are the rules. You gotta finish that one, then go pour another one and then finish that as well. Aliyah made the rule that you have to drink double."

"That's a joke." Dad said as he downed the glass of scotch. He coughed a few times. "It only burned a little," he mumbled, walked over to the bench, and poured himself another glass of straight scotch. He downed that one, before pouring a third glass and returning to sit at the table. He looked straight at Aliyah.

"Just you wait," he warned.

Ben drew another card, a ten of diamonds.

"Categories, hmmmm." He paused, before saying, "Brands of cars. I'll start with *Ford.*"

"*Holden,*" I said.

"*Peugeot,*" Aliyah added.

"*Toyota,*" said Dad.

"*Mitsubishi,*" said Ben.

This one went around the table for a few rounds before stopping at Aliyah.

"Uhhhh, ummmmm," she stalled.

"Drink!" we all demanded, thumping the table.

Aliyah took a drink and placed her glass back on the table.

"Your turn, Brendan," she said.

I drew from the pile. "It's a five."

"What's that again?" Dad asked.

"Thumbs," we cohesively said.

"That is?" he asked.

"Whenever Brendan rests his thumb on the table, you must copy. The last to do so drinks." Aliyah added as she grabbed another card.

"Another jack. Well, I keep the rule the same."

Dad drew a card and pinned it to his chest. He extended it a tiny bit to get a sneak peek.

"Get stuffed," he said as flicked the card to the other side of the room.

"What was it?" we asked.

"Not important," he responded as he skulled his scotch. He proceeded to stand up, pour another, and then he skulled that.

Aliyah laughed. "You are in for a messy night at this rate."

Dad came back with another glass. "Just someone draw a jack soon, please."

We went around the table again, all drawing cards. I kid you not, Dad drew a third eight. That's six scotches in the space of ten minutes. He sat down after his scotches and the signs were beginning to show. I have never seen someone have such bad luck in one game.

"You ready?" asked Ben.

Dad nodded.

You could always tell when Dad was drunk, he had to close his eyes to do anything that required thinking or talking. That was why he shut his eyes when he nodded.

Ben drew his card. "Four!" he shouted as he dropped to the floor.

Aliyah and I followed suit leaving Dad sitting on the

chair.

"What's four?" Dad asked.

"Four to the floor," Ben answered.

"What?" he asked.

"All four limbs on the floor!" I shouted.

Dad dropped to the floor straight away, not realizing he would have to drink anyway. Dad hit the floor so hard his face bounced off the floorboards.

"Oh, shit," I said.

We all jumped off the floor to help him.

"Are you okay?" Aliyah asked.

"All good," Dad responded.

We helped him to his feet.

"Your lip's bleeding!" I said.

Dad touched his lip with his fingers and looked at the blood on them. All he did was shrug. "The show must go on," he said as he took another drink. "Whose turn is it?" he asked.

We followed the table around until it got to Dad.

He drew a king, "Yes!" he screamed as he jumped out of the chair with both hands in the air. "That's the final king, isn't it?"

"Yeah! Why?" Aliyah questioned.

"Because that means I win!" He slammed the card on the table and began to walk off.

We were all laughing.

"Bill," Aliyah said, "the fourth king loses and has to drink the whole cup."

Dad looked at us unable to stand up straight and keep his balance.

"No, King's Cup, king is the winner, others drink cup." Dad laughed with that exact wording.

"No king is loser, last king drawn, drinks cup," I corrected.

Dad just stopped with a blank look on his face. "Seriously?" he asked.

We all kept laughing.

To his credit, Dad drank all the cup had to offer. I walked upstairs to get Mum. We walked downstairs to see Aliyah and Ben laughing their heads off while watching Dad on the gym equipment.

"Weeee," he shouted as he lay face down on the gym ball with his arms stretched out. "I'm Superman!"

He fell off the ball and onto the ground. Mum helped him up to his feet.

"Time for bed," she said as they walked upstairs slowly. Mum turned around and looked down at us. "Why is his lip bleeding?"

"It's a long story, Mum," I said.

"Well, don't get up to too much mischief. I love you all. Good night!"

We all managed a mixture of "Good night," and "Love you, too," before making our own way to bed.

CHAPTER SEVEN: THE NEW YEAR

I was sitting at home reading some study material. It was four in the afternoon on a miserable summer's day, January fourth to be exact. My phone started ringing. It was Aliyah.

"What can I do for you, beautiful?" I asked.

"Babe!" said Aliyah.

I could hear the overwhelming amount of excitement coming through.

"I kind of got a traineeship with a fashion designer." Her excitement never wavered. "It's a place out near the beach, really renowned for not only their styles, but also the personal assistants they produce."

"Holy crap, babe, that's so amazing!" I was genuinely happy for her. "Maybe get your butt home so I can take you out for dinner?" I asked.

I heard a hmmm on the other end of the phone. "Nah," she said.

"The attitude, babe, so sassy!" I replied. I heard a giggle on the other end of the line. "No, but seriously, I'm taking you out for dinner to celebrate. What do you feel like?"

"I'd love some Thai. Can we make this a family event?" Aliyah asked.

"Of course."

We went to dinner at a small Thai restaurant in town. The restaurant was a squeeze. It was like a corridor, lucky to fit five people seated across, but it worked. It was packed. Although her whole family was there, I was so happy for her.

"So," I said to Aliyah, "tell me what happened, step-by-step." Aliyah took a breath to begin but I quickly cut her off. "Don't leave anything out, either."

"I walked in and spoke to the receptionist. Her name is Yvonne. I handed her resume and asked her if she could pass it onto her boss. She told me that they were looking for a trainee, but she would let me know. I would have loved to talk the owner, but the place was absolutely packed. They must have been preparing for a show. We just moved on to shopping, as it was the last location of the day where we handed in a resume. Anyway, like an hour into shopping, I get a call. It turned out to be Alexander who owns the place, and I start Monday!"

"There you have it." I stretched my arm out to hold hers on the other side of the table. "Congratulations, babe. I'm very proud of my girl."

Aliyah and I gazed at each other with big smiles. "I love you!" I mouthed to her across the table.

"I love you more," she mouthed back.

Our moment was interrupted by Mark's girlfriend, Hannah. "So, what will you do?" she asked.

"Hopefully I love it, and I can use my traineeship as a stepping stone in my career. If not, I plan on deferring university, and I'll know by next year whether to continue or to quit and follow the university path."

"That makes sense," Hannah replied.

"You've always been amazing with your fashion sense and styling. I think you'll be great at it," chimed in her brother, Andy.

"Thank you. I hope so! Now enough about me. Let's enjoy some beautiful Thai," Aliyah replied just as our entrees arrived and damn those spring rolls smelled delicious

"Happy two-year anniversary!" Aliyah shouted. As I

slowly opened my eyes, I could see her oozing with excitement. It was contagious. It didn't take me long to sit up and enjoy the moment with her. She reached down beside the bed to grab a perfectly wrapped parcel.

"No, no, no!" I exclaimed. "You said no presents."

"Too bad!" she said, cheekily grinning from ear to ear, "Now open it."

By that point, she was kneeling on the bed beside me. I sat with my back against the headboard. She was still as excited as ever. It was a quality I always loved about her. She always went the extra mile to make someone's day a little bit more special, but it was always genuine.

Aliyah hit me on the shoulder. "Open it!"

I looked her dead in the eye. I knew I was frustrating her. "I love you," I replied.

She hit me again. "Cool story. Now open it!"

I unwrapped my present painfully slow, grinning and watching Aliyah out of the corner of my eye. I paused, turned, and looked straight at her.

"No way!" I exclaimed. Now as excited as Aliyah had been, I stopped playing games and ripped the parcel open. "Thank you so much!" I said as I kissed Aliyah on the cheek. It was a blazer I had seen recently in the shops but didn't have the money to buy at the time.

"Did you notice the other present?" she asked.

"You didn't get me another present, did you?" I asked.

"They were wrapped together."

I rummaged through the plastic wrapping I had thrown off the bed. There it was. I picked it up and held it out in front of me.

"Should I be told something?"

"Not at all. It was just cute, and it matched your top."

In front of me, I held an identical tiny version of the blazer.

"I just love it. It matches yours, and we can start a baby drawer," Aliyah said, grabbing the mini-blazer out of my hands.

"You actually spoil me." I kissed Aliyah on the cheek, leaned down beside the bed, and picked up a poorly wrapped parcel. I handed it to her. She shook the parcel next to her ear trying to figure out what it was.

"I thought you didn't get me a present," she said.

"As if, mate," I replied.

"It feels weird," Aliyah said while holding the parcel.

I nodded, "I wrapped it oddly to throw you off."

Aliyah opened her present.

"I love it!" She pulled out black and white cheetah print shoes, along with some leggings to go with them.

"Should I be told something?" Aliyah asked as she laughed while holding the leggings up in front of her.

"Yeah, take a hint," I answered with a serious look on my face.

Aliyah gasped. She was shocked. The look on her face said it all. She hit me on the arm very hard. "Too far," she muttered as she pulled the final part of her present from the wrapping.

It was a gold body chain. "I love them all so much." She wrapped her arms around me.

"I just thought dance might clash with your new work schedule. You're always talking about getting into the gym and running a bit more. It wasn't too hard to choose. I mean all three were all saved on my phone."

Aliyah laughed. "My subtle hints are working, are they? What about the body chain?" she asked.

"You said something about how one of your co-dancers was wearing one, so thought I'd give it a crack and see if you like it."

"I love it." She snuggled up to me.

"Now pack your gear."

"Why?" Aliyah asked.

"Because we're going away for a few nights, to celebrate, of course."

"Is this why you hadn't bought the blazer?" Aliyah asked.

"Not at all, now go."

"Thank you," she whispered in my ear as she cuddled me.

The excitement returned to her as she raced out of bed.

"How long do I have?" she asked while flicking through her clothes rack.

"Don't stress, babe. You have at least two hours. No hurry at all."

Aliyah took her head out of her wardrobe and look straight at me. She pointed at me and yelled in a high pitch tone, "Don't you tell me not to stress!"

She had that real serious look on her face, much different to the look of excitement and the joy-filled smile she'd had all morning. Aliyah immediately turned her attention back to her cupboard. Under her breathe, she was muttering, "What to wear, what to wear," while frantically looking through her clothes. I hopped out of my bed and packed mine.

Two hours had passed, and the car was loaded, ready for us to leave. We said goodbye to our family members and hopped in the car. We were listening to the standard songs on the radio when I asked Aliyah what she was doing.

"Nothing?" she replied with a real serious look on her face. She didn't know whether to be confused or angry over my question.

"What are you doing?" I asked again. Aliyah looked at me even more confused than the first time.

"Nothing," she repeated, looking puzzled.

"Exactly! Where is DJ Aliyah?"

"Oh, right! My bad." She put her phone down as if she never had any music on it. "Where's your phone?"

I reached into my pocket and handed her mine.

"Let it begin." She plugged the phone into the aux cord.

We arrived at our hotel, checked into our room, and left our gear there. The hotel backed onto a golf course and a nature reserve. It was loaded with bush trails and great outdoor activities that we loved. We scoped around the place before driving back into the main town to see what it had to offer. Neither Aliyah nor I had spent much time there. The town was decently big, one hundred thousand people was a pretty close estimate. We drove right into the centre of town until we found a venue.

"Over there!" Aliyah pointed.

I turned my head to see a spot for glow in the dark mini-golf. There wasn't even a question, a nod, or a conversation. The decision to play glow in the dark mini-golf would be unanimous. We parked the car and walked inside.

We were greeted by a lady at the counter. She was older, maybe mid-forties, larger, dark hair and eyes, but very friendly. "How are you today?" she asked.

"Very well, thank you!" Aliyah replied.

"How are you?" I asked.

"Work is so and so, but it's always nice serving people with smiles." She paused for a moment. "Now was it just a game for two?"

We both nodded.

"Choose your color golf balls." She gestured to the basket.

Aliyah and I peered into the basket. There were a lot of the golf balls that were fluorescent to help see in the dark. Aliyah grabbed a bright orange while I grabbed a bright yellow.

"Why yellow?" Aliyah asked.

"Because pink is too close to orange."

We turned back to the lady to see her holding two putters. She handed them to us. She reached down and grabbed a piece of paper and a pencil.

"Here's your scorecard and your pencil. Make sure you have a fun time." She pointed to the hallway.

It was dark in that direction.

"Thank you," we said simultaneously.

We walked down the hallway arm in arm with our clubs in our outside hands. We arrived at the first hole. It was so cool. Aliyah was bent over with the scorecard, writing out names in the boxes. I was sussing out the course.

"Let's make this interesting. Loser buys dinner," I said.

Aliyah laughed. "I'll be sure not to drain your bank account, but I'm pretty hungry."

"So sassy, babe, I love it. Come give me a kiss." Aliyah walked to me, and at the last moment, turned away laughing. "Do you start or do I?" I asked looking at the course.

"Guess you can then," Aliyah said doing her best to pretend that didn't happen.

She gave me a tap on the ass as I walked over to the first hole. I hit it hard, it ricocheted right off two obstacles almost directly back onto the starting mat.

"Great start, babe." Aliyah snickered.

"You can talk when you do better," I said with my head down, lining up for my next stroke. I struck the ball with less power but got the same result. I didn't mind much. I knew Aliyah would need help. I decided to play it safe and putt around the obstacles. I sunk the ball.

"That's five," Aliyah acknowledged while writing in my score on the card.

"Now watch and learn." Aliyah took to the tee, so to speak. She walked to the first hole.

"What are you doing?"

"Calculating."

"Why? How? You can barely see."

Aliyah raised her index finger to her lips. "Shhhh."

I did. I stood there and watched. She hit the ball with minimal power. It bounced off two walls and went in. A hole in one. She jumped in the air with her golf club above her head in her outstretched arms.

"Hole in one. Hole in one," she chanted. She gave me a hug. I had half a mind to brush past her and keep the rivalry going, but truth is I was happy for her. I lifted her up by the waist, and she cheered even louder. I put her feet back on the ground.

"You're still going to lose." I walked over to the tee.

We played the next sixteen holes. The dark made for an experience.

"Last hole," Aliyah said as we arrived at the tee.

"What's the score?"

"You're down by two. You've got no chance."

The last hole looked very simple, but it must have been deceiving. It was a dead straight course and about a ten-meter putt. At the end was a big rock with a tiny hole in the bottom center. If you made the tunnel, it was an automatic hole in one. If you missed it, you pretty much end up back where you started because it was uphill besides the last meter being flat. I played it safe. I putted gently to the rock and sank my putt in two strokes. Aliyah, however, tried to hit the tunnel on her first swing. Just like I had hoped. The shot literally just missed and bounced back towards us.

"Pressure's on now," I joked. "Only two more shots to win. Don't choke."

I could tell Aliyah was trying to block me out. I walked up close to her and whispered in her ear. "Don't choke, don't choke."

"I'll take pasta of some sort and a chick-flick, thanks," she said, handing me her golf club.

"Oi, come back here,"

Aliyah turned around, ran, and jumped on me. She wrapped her arms around my neck and her legs around my waist. We both had the biggest smiles on our face.

"I love you," I whispered.

"I'll always love you more," she whispered back.

We walked out of the course swinging our arms.

"Who won?" the lady asked us.

"Winners don't matter, just as long as we had fun," I said.

Aliyah looked directly at me, "That's what losers say."

We handed our clubs to the lady at the counter and hopped back into the car.

"Are you sure on the pasta?" I asked.

"One hundred percent. I don't know what I want, though, between Gnocchi and Carbonara!"

"Porque no los dos?"

Aliyah laughed, "Yeah all right, we'll grab both."

We ended up grabbing our take away meals from a local pub and headed back to our hotel to watch the movies.

"What's your choice?" I flicked through the selection.

"I'm not sure," she replied. "Keep scrolling!" "Ooo! Ooo! Stop!" she said all excitedly. "Go back!"

"To what?" I asked. It was the usual chick flick. "Are you sure?" I asked in a very condescending tone.

She punched me on the shoulder. "Put it on."

We ate our dinner and watched part of the movie. It was standard for her to fall asleep during a movie, every time without fail, and want to watch it the next day. I turned the movie off and admired the girl who fell asleep on my chest. Every day she had become ever more beautiful.

The next morning we woke incredibly early, even before the sun. It was nice to watch the end of the movie as the sun rays slowly crept in through our window. We decided it was time to get up and enjoy a nice morning walk at the local waterfalls. It was still very fresh outside. The ground was nice and dewy, and nature smelled amazing.

CHAPTER EIGHT: PHYSICALLY BATTERED, EMOTIONALLY SATISFIED

I was still playing locally. For our eleventh game of the season, we were taking on our division rivals. It didn't look like a promising day for us, but as a team, we all wanted to show up and do our best. We never minded the scoreboard at the end of the day. We just enjoyed running out there with our mates. I always got the tough job on defence. I say that because when constantly losing—sometimes by a fair margin, week-in-week-out—your opponent constantly got a lot of perfect deliveries with no pressure. Not to mention the fact that the position generally attracted players who were a good five to six inches taller than me and weighed twenty kilograms more.

That day was no exception. I was on the leading goalkicker, Steven Bryce. I figured the only way to play him was to not even touch him, but rather clog the holes he tried to lead into. Kind of like a zone defense. It worked for a good ten minutes as he hadn't touched the ball yet. When a deep ball headed our way, I got a fist in and brought the ball to the ground. As I did, I landed in an awkward split position. When you're not flexible, that hurts the groin enough as it is. I wasn't stable, but that became the least of my worries. Steven Bryce, all one-hundred-and-ten kilograms of him came down on top of my left knee. My body jerked into the fetal position and I clutched my knee with both hands in agony. The play went on around us. They ended up scoring their first goal for the match. Once the play had finished, Steven jogged over to check up on me.

He didn't even wait for a response before signaling for the medical staff. They hurried out quickly and play had to stop. The medical team carried me off the field, down the race, and into the rooms. They sat me on the table and began to assess the injury.

"How are you feeling, mate?" Hayley asked me. Hayley and I had developed a bond over the years. I considered her more of a friend than just our medical trainer.

"My day is definitely done, I heard a pop," I responded.

Hayley's face dropped. She always knew how honest I was and how I usually tried to play through any injury. A lot of the guys would come off the training track for a free massage or always sought treatment at quarter-time or half-time. She always loved when I came to her, knowing she had something to genuinely treat. My pain started to disappear but that was what worried me the most. I could hear my Dad's voice reminiscing of his days where he had to have a knee reconstruction.

"ACL's were always the most painful injury in the world," he'd said often, "but after a couple of minutes, you start to question whether you were hurt. You could even go run a marathon."

Hayley started trying to twist my knee to find a sore spot. "Are you in any pain?" she asked.

I shook my head. I could see the doubt in her face, although she tried her best to remain positive.

"Up you get, let's run some tests then." She helped me up, and we walked into the warm-up room. "Let's walk in a straight line."

I did. For a few minutes, we paced back and forth, being very cautious of my knee.

"Seems good. Let's do some very light jogging," Hayley

instructed.

We did that, too, very, very light, to one end of the room and back again. Hayley ran beside me the whole time. We slowly picked up the pace every time we turned until we almost had a full sprint going. Our room was thirty meters long, so we could build up a decent stride.

"How's that feel?" she asked.

"Perfect," I said with the biggest smile on my face. I guess I got caught up in the moment because Hayley wasn't the slightest bit convinced. After all, she was the professional.

"There's a test I need to run. If it's what I think it is, you'll end up back on the floor in pain again. However, you can't go back on the field if I don't run it."

Hayley had her hands on her hips, she looked genuinely upset. As I said we had become close over our seasons together. She could tell I was hurt.

I nodded reluctantly. "Guess we should give it a go."

"Ok, mirror what I do." Hayley began to jog slowly on the spot. I copied. We picked up the speed to the fastest we could. We pushed the right leg out laterally before pushing off it, back to our center and kept jogging.

"How'd the feel?" she asked.

"Good."

We kept jogging. We put the left leg out a tiny margin before pushing off it back to our starting jogging on the spot.

"Good or bad?" she asked.

"Yeah, all right."

"Okay, go a bit further this time." She said.

I kept jogging before pushing my left leg out and pushing off it back to my starting spot.

"Any luck?" she asked.

"A bit sore, but I should be okay."

We jogged for a bit longer.

"This one could hurt, but load it right up with no hesitation," she directed.

We kept jogging for a moment before I loaded my left knee right up. It buckled underneath me, and I was back on the floor. I slid myself over to the wall and sat up with my back against it. Hayley came and sat beside me. We didn't say a word. It was just silence. After a few minutes, Hayley got up and walked over to grab me some ice.

"Guess it's time to rehabilitate," she said. She grabbed the cling wrap and wrapped the ice to the inside of my knee. At first, it felt worse than doing the injury itself, but over time the pain began to disappear.

"Do you need me to call you an ambulance to take you to casualty?" she asked.

I glanced at her, very confused. "Casualty?" I asked.

"Sorry, emergency. We always called it casualty in my day."

I reshuffled the ice on my leg as my knee was getting numb. "Is that my only option? I don't want to sit there for ages."

"I'd honestly recommend going home and getting a good night's rest. Go to the physio in the morning and let them assess you."

I nodded. "Yeah, I'll do that."

"Can I get you anything else?"

"Actually, can you go into the black bag and throw me my phone? I might as well check the footy scores."

Hayley passed my phone to me before leaving the room. She had to go check on the bench to ensure no one else was hurt. I dialed Aliyah's number. She answered hesitantly.

"Hello?" she said. I could hear the confused undertone even from the other end of the line.

"I didn't think you would answer during dance," I responded.

"You should be playing football. I figured it was an emergency. What's up?"

"I just wanted to apologize. I can't do date night tonight. I've hurt my knee pretty bad."

"I'm coming straight there."

Aliyah hung up before even giving me a chance to argue. I tried calling back a few times. I never wanted her to leave her dance rehearsal. I just didn't want her to be too disappointed at six-thirty when she finished and couldn't go on the date. It didn't take long for Aliyah to walk through the doors with Hayley. They helped me to my feet. Once I stood up, I could bear weight on my knee again. That scared me the most. All I could hear in the back of my mind was Dad's voice on replay. I couldn't shake that thought out of my head that it was an ACL. I didn't want surgery. I didn't want time off work. I wanted to be ok. I sat in the car and thanked Hayley before Aliyah took me home.

We arrived home, and I hobbled up the driveway on crutches Hayley found for me. Aliyah rushed inside, made the bed and fluffed the pillows. She helped me to bed. "What happened?" she asked.

I explained the story to her. I could tell from her facial reactions she was visualizing the incident in her head.

"Do you know the damage?" she asked as she wrapped her arms around me.

I shook my head. I felt the tears welling in my eyes as my head was bowed down. My throat got all croaky. "I just hope it isn't an ACL."

Silence swept the room. Aliyah tightened her grip around me but didn't say a word. After about a minute she spoke. "Let's just try to have a good night, and we will go to the physio in the morning. No point ruining our night now." She paused for a moment. "Where's your phone?"

I passed my phone to her. "I'm going to set you an alarm for every hour, so I can grab you an icepack."

That was what she did all night, without fail. She helped me reposition and place the icepack accordingly and let me fall asleep, before taking it off after fifteen minutes and putting it back in the freezer. She grabbed any water or food when necessary. She genuinely cared for my well-being.

I barely got any sleep that night. Whenever I tried to move, my knee would lock into a painful position, and I lay silently trying not to wake Aliyah. The morning came around slowly, but Aliyah didn't waste a minute. She was straight on the phone to book my physio appointment.

"Yes, yes, we can be there in ten minutes. Okay, yep, see you soon." She hung up the phone and grabbed my crutches.

"You hobble slowly to the car and wait for me. I'll pack everything you need."

We arrived at the sports clinic, greeted by a young blonde receptionist who had a coffee in one hand and had barely made any effort to get dressed. Her hair looked like it had been in a windstorm, and she could barely keep her eyes open.

"Big night?" I asked as I hobbled to the counter.

"Best friend's twenty-first," she mumbled as she took another sip from her coffee cup. "Brendan, was it?"

I nodded.

"It's sad that I'm still in a better state than you."

I could see the empathy on her face as she made that remark. It was like she had seen too many of those injuries, time and time before.

"I just need your player membership card, then follow the corridor there. It's the first door on your left." Aliyah dug through my wallet and handed her my membership card.

We made our way down the corridor slowly, admiring the framed memorabilia of sporting legends on the wall. We reached the room, where we were greeted by James. James seemed like a nice bloke. He was thirty-odd years old, brown hair spiked up, roughly five-foot-six-inches tall. He seemed like he hadn't been a physio long but had a high level of professionalism about him.

"Brendan, is it?" He greeted me with his outstretched hand. I had to balance on one of my crutches as I shook his. He turned to Aliyah. "You are?" he asked with an outstretched hand.

"Aliyah," she said.

"Ahh, his carer," he joked, smiling. James gestured to the table behind him. "Come take a seat and tell me what happened."

I told him the whole incident, from the beginning. He took notes down on his pad before he got me to lie back and begin his evaluation.

"Now bring your foot to your bottom but still have it planted on the table, just so your knee is raised." James grasped my knee and jerked my leg towards him. "Are you okay?" he asked. He could clearly see that my whole body had tensed up.

"It doesn't hurt nearly as much as I thought it would," I replied. "I was probably just anticipating much more pain than there really was."

James ran a few more tests, poking and prodding, pushing and pulling.

"What's the verdict?" I asked.

"I can't tell. There's too much swelling around the injury to get a definitive answer. You'll have to get an MRI."

My face had dropped by then. That's never good news. "No gut feeling?" I asked.

"I haven't dealt with many ACL's before."

My heart sank, no one ever starts a sentence like that without it being relevant.

"But with the lack of movement, how you told me the incident occurred and not to mention the pop—"

I cut James off mid-sentence. "I'm ninety-nine percent certain the pop was from my hip."

I wasn't trying to be rude—I just didn't want to believe it was my ACL.

James continued. "As I said, with the incident and the pop, during the time no one can really know where the pop came from. If it looks like a duck and sounds like a duck, it's probably is a duck. We won't be able to tell until your MRI results get back due to the swelling." James tapped me on my good leg. "Whenever you're ready, jump up."

He walked over to his desk and began to write more notes. Aliyah helped me stabilize myself on my crutches. He wrote me a note for the MRI. "You're probably best off going to the one down the street. They have the shortest wait time. Call them tomorrow, book your appointment, and they'll send the results through within a few days. I'll give you a buzz when I receive them."

"Thank you," I said.

"Good luck," were his parting words. He followed us down the hallway to the waiting room.

"Joel," he announced, looking at a little kid roughly eleven years old. He had his arm in a sling and looked defeated much like me.

"Do I need to sign anything else?" I asked the receptionist.

"Not at all, good luck with the MRI."

She had said that with a smile. Maybe her morning coffee had finally kicked in. It was the first sign of life I had seen in her.

"Thank you, have a nice day," I said.

We left the clinic and made our way to the car. Aliyah helped me get in before sitting in the driver's seat.

She turned to face me. "Are you okay?"

I nodded.

"Are you sure?" she asked.

"I'll be fine," I replied.

I could tell she didn't believe me. It could be the fact that she knows me better than anyone else, or it could be the fact that it was said with an unconvincing smile.

Aliyah started the car. "What do you want to do?" she asked.

"Honestly?" Aliyah just stared at me, as if she was waiting for the response. "I just need to go home and lay in bed."

"Done."

It made me smile that she never hesitated. She was the best kind of girlfriend, the best friend. She always wanted to put my needs before hers. The one that always looked after me, just wanted to see me smile.

Monday morning came quickly, and I woke to Aliyah booking my MRI appointment.

The door shut behind her as she came back into the room. "You'll have to get ready, your MRI is in thirty minutes."

We hopped to the car and drove to the clinic. It was fifteen minutes of silence.

Aliyah parked the car and grabbed my hand. "You're going to be okay."

I tried to smile, but I couldn't. I was too nervous.

"I'm going to be with you every step. I got you," she promised, took a deep breath, and kissed my hand. "You've got this, babe."

It took me a while to hobble into the clinic, but I was one of the first in there so there was no wait time. I had to lay incredibly still in the machine. I always wondered how people with claustrophobia would do it. It's difficult to lie in one spot, especially when you need to lay in a certain position for them to take photos of your knee. It's even worse when that position is uncomfortable and borderline painful. It eventually finished, and we made our way back to the car.

"Nervous?" Aliyah asked me.

I nodded while staring at the floor. I probably looked defeated. I was defeated. I didn't say much for the rest of the day. I knew it upset her to see me like that, but she didn't show it. She tried her best to make me smile on the odd occasion.

Wednesday morning, the phone ringing woke me.

Aliyah answered. "Hello, Aliyah speaking."

She covered the bottom of the phone and whispered to me. "It's for you. They have your test results in."

I reached out my hand. Aliyah passed me the phone.

"This is Brendan speaking."

"Hello, Brendan. It's James from the physio. How are you today?"

"I'm doing very well thanks. Yourself?"

"Yeah, not too bad. I have your test results here. Turns out it's a grade two strain on your MCL. At least it's not as bad as it could've been."

I took a deep breath. I was thankful. It was a sigh of relief.

Aliyah cradled on my shoulder for a moment of silence.

"Hello, Brendan. Are you still there?" James asked.

"Yeah, sorry."

"Are you okay?" he asked.

"Relieved more than anything."

"That's fair enough. It's a good result. I would like you to stay on bedrest till Monday. Ice as much as you can. Try to remember you're trying to remove all the swelling. Then on Monday, I will book you in for a nine-thirty session so we can begin your rehabilitation."

"Sounds brilliant."

"Any other questions?"

"James, how long will my rehabilitation take?"

"Depending on your commitment to the rehab, you will have full mobility in your knee in approximately six weeks."

"That's brilliant!" I said with a huge grin.

"But for now, rest and I will see you on Monday."

I hung up the phone and placed it on the bed. Aliyah stared at me with the cutest smile.

"So?" she asked.

"What?"

"How do you go?" she asked before I even got a chance to answer the question. "What'd he say?"

"I have a grade two strain on my MCL. Six weeks, I hope."

Aliyah hit my arm with excitement and kissed me on the cheek.

"That's brilliant! I'm so happy right now. What happens next?"

"I have to keep resting until Monday."

Aliyah smiled. "Lucky I took the whole week off work."

Chapter Nine: A Bright Future

The next few weeks were very painful. The journey began with lots of ultrasound on the swollen knee and slowly being able to bear as much weight as possible. I made my way to short distance running. The pain was scary. There's always that gremlin in the back of my mind worrying I would re-injure my knee. Every step of the way, and every time I had a doubt, Aliyah was there. Picking me up when I fell, making me do my extra work even when I didn't feel like it, reassuring me that everything would be okay, and it would be worth it. It made me seriously reconsider all my life choices. Did I want to play footy and risk reinjuring it? Where was my career going if I kept taking time off? There were so many unanswered ones, but I knew one thing for certain. I wanted to marry my best friend. It was all going to be fine if I get to come home to her smile every day. I wasn't fazed on our ages being as young as we were. I just knew I needed her in my life.

I waited until Wednesday night when I knew she would be home late. I was doing the dishes when Trevor asked me how my knee was traveling.

"Every morning is a struggle to move, but once I complete my exercises it seems to be all right."

"Are you going to make it back in time for any games?" Susan asked.

"I don't know if I will go back," I replied.

Trevor and Susan both looked at me, their faces smeared in shock and disbelief.

"Don't go making rash decisions," said Trevor.

"Yeah," agreed Susan, "you've always been a brilliant player since you were young. Don't give up on something because of one horrible incident."

"Thanks, guys," I said, "but this injury has thrown a few things into perspective. I want to be a dad more than anything in this world. To go with that, I want to be able to run around and kick the footy with my kids and play catch. The more injuries I sustain the less chance I have of that. It's time for me to finally head to university and begin a career path in business. Maybe someday I'll own those warehouses that I'm working for."

A moment of silence swept the room. I guess they could see how serious I was. How quickly this injury had shaped my perspective. I guess they could tell my decision had been made.

"Plus," I continued. "I got off lucky with this injury. If it was an ACL or worse, I'd be out of work for quite some time and have a big surgery bill to go with it. That doesn't help set me up for my future, a future I really hope your daughter wants to be a part of."

Trevor and Susan's eyes lit up. "What are you saying?" Trevor asked.

"I want to marry your daughter. I'd like permission from both of you, as your opinions mean a lot to me."

Trevor and Susan both embraced me.

"Of course," said Susan.

"Thanks for asking, but you never needed to. Nothing would make us smile more than seeing the two of you get married." Trevor gently added. I could hear the crackles in his voice, the emotion behind his words. "May I ask why, though?"

"My whole day is good or bad based on her. She always brings a smile to my face when I wake up, and I know everything will be okay if I get to come home to her. The last few weeks, she has been looking after me while I was injured proved she's my absolute rock, and as long as she's by my side, I know everything will be okay."

Susan held her arms clasped to her chest while Trevor laughed. "You big cutie," he said with a smile on his face.

"What are you going to do for a ring?" Susan asked.

"I was hoping you would like to come shopping with me? Will you?" I asked Susan.

"When are we going?" She asked.

"Aliyah has to work every Saturday morning. I figured we could go then."

"Sounds like a plan," she responded. "Any ideas on the ring?"

"Well, my online account has many, many, great rings and wedding dress ideas. I'm sure we will get a few good ideas from there. Right now, I'm thinking a plain band with three diamonds, with a colored diamond centerpiece."

Susan nodded her head, "I can see it now, and I love it. Simple yet elegant."

Susan and Trevor both hugged me.

"This is so exciting," Trevor said. "You're getting married."

They both smiled.

"She has to say yes, first," I added.

"Brendan . . ." Trevor paused for a moment. "Come on, mate, as if she won't."

The front door slammed shut. Trevor and Susan immediately went back to doing the dishes, and I sat down on the stool. We could all hear a few faint crashes before Aliyah appeared in the hallway, heading to the kitchen. I stood up to greet her with open arms. She walked down and wrapped herself up in them.

"What were you guys doing? You all look so guilty," she

said.

"Drugs," I replied.

Aliyah gave me a weird look.

"We built a car, too," Susan snickered.

"Don't forget about the stock market crash course we all took," Trevor added.

"You're all such smart asses," she responded.

"How was work?" I asked.

"Long and tiring. I'm starving. What's for dinner?" Aliyah walked over to the stove. "I love enchiladas."

Saturday morning came around a lot quicker than we expected. It was time to begin ring shopping.

"Where do you want to start?" Susan asked me.

"I'm thinking there will be plenty of jewelers right in the heart of the city."

On the drive up, I watched a video on my phone of the recent volcano eruption in Hawaii. "I'm just glad we don't live near a volcano."

Susan turned to look at me.

"What?" I asked.

"The Moss Twins."

"What about them?"

"The Moss Twins are volcanoes, not active, but they're volcanoes."

I could not contain my fits of laughter. "Who the hell told you that?" I asked.

"We learned it in primary school. Everybody got taught it."

"You believed it? With no research whatsoever?"

"Why did you doubt it?"

"I've been to the top of the Moss twins. A lot of people have. They're just mountains."

"I'm being serious," Susan stated.

"Okay, hold up. How about I google it?" I pulled out my phone. Google led me to a website dedicated to the history of our city.

"Can't wait for you to swallow your words," Susan remarked in a smug tone.

"I ain't swallowing shit," I replied. "Here it is, contrary to the popular belief, the Moss Twins are not volcanoes. Do I read on?" I questioned.

"Bullshit," Susan responded.

I handed her the phone. "Here, I'll take the wheel."

Susan took the phone from my hands while I put my hand on the steering wheel. She scrolled through the phone.

"I was so confident. I've always believed that." Susan threw the phone back on my lap and put her hands on the wheel. "You can't tell anyone. I don't want them thinking I'm stupid."

I started laughing. "Oh, trust me, I'm telling everyone."

We parked the car and walked around.

"Are you confident you know what you're looking for?" Susan asked.

"I don't really know, but I'm banking I'll know when I see it."

We stopped off at a jeweller. I saw a big plain diamond ring on a gold band. We walked in to inquire, and the lady took the ring out of the casing and put it on the table.

"The ring has just over a one-carat diamond with an eighteen-carat gold band. It's simple and elegant," she added.

I put the ring on my pinkie finger. "How much?" I asked.

"Seventeen thousand."

I was shocked. It looked like engagement ring shopping was going to be expensive.

"What are you thinking?" Susan asked.

"Not the one," I said. "I don't think plain is what I'm

after."

We walked down the street to the next jewelry store, one a little more elegant.

"Hello, welcome to our store. My name is Kate. Would you like to take a seat?" Kate gestured to two chairs at a table with a glass top. We sat down while Kate bought us over some brochures.

"Do you know what you're after?" she asked.

"I'm just browsing, to be honest. I kind of have an idea in my mind but wanted to see some rings in person."

"Well," Kate laughed, "you've come to the wrong place for browsing. We make all our rings and cater to the clients wants and needs. I can show you some key areas to look for quickly, if you'd like?"

"I'd really appreciate that."

"The first rule when shopping is to remember the four Cs, color, clarity, cut, and carat. You also need to be very smart. Are you planning on spending much?"

"A little over five."

"You can find a nice ring for that price," Kate said, nodding. "That price, there are a few little tricks though. For example, the difference between a one-carat ring and a .90 carat ring isn't too visible to people. The price is, though."

"Why?" I asked. I was deeply browsing into the brochure she had handed me.

"Obviously, the bigger diamond, the rarer to mine. You can, however, go down on the level of clarity to afford a bigger diamond." Kate started looking in her case, then pulled out two sample rings.

"I'm no diamond evaluator, but can you tell me the difference between these two rings?" Kate handed me the rings. "One is a flawless cut, the other a SI."

I studied both rings for a moment.

"I wouldn't be able to tell," Susan said, while leaning over my shoulder.

I handed the ring back to Kate. "There's a slight difference, but only noticeable because they're next to each other," I said.

Kate put the rings back in the case and took out two more. "Big differences can be noticeable, but not too much to the naked eye." Kate handed me a ring. "This is H on the colour scale."

"That's a nice ring."

"Yeah, it is, but can you see the color stain?" Kate asked.

I shook my head. Kate handed me a second ring. "That's a D."

"Well again, I can't tell until you put them side by side."

"Most people can't," she said.

I handed her back the rings. Susan and I stood up. Kate walked us to the door. I shook Kate's hand.

"Thank you so much. If we decide to get a ring made, I'll be straight to your doorstep."

"Thank you," Kate said. "I hope I helped."

"Like you wouldn't believe," I said as we walked out of the store.

Susan and I continued our journey through the city.

"What are you thinking?" she asked.

"Lunch would be brilliant," I replied.

Susan smirked. "You're an idiot. I meant about the ring."

"I'm aware."

Silence was all that was left from that conversation. We continued to walk down main street.

"Well?" Susan asked.

"Well, what?" I replied with a grin on my face.

"You're a real smart ass sometimes, Brendan!" There was another moment of silence. "Seriously, tell me." Susan shook my shoulder. Although playfully, I could sense her frustration.

"After seeing a few rings, I think I will definitely go with the three diamonds on the plain band setting with a light blue or purple colored diamond in the middle."

Susan nodded.

"It's nice to get some tips and tricks. A colored diamond will cut out most of the clarity cost, and the triple stones will always look brilliant. She will love it. This is so exciting."

"Now as for the most important thing of the day. I'm thinking of a kebab for lunch." I stated.

Susan shook her head. "Yeah, all right, a kebab sounds good."

We grabbed our lunch from a corner shop and sat at wooden picnic tables.

"You're one hundred percent certain you want to marry my daughter?"

I smiled and nodded.

"Because rings and marriages are expensive."

"I'm aware," I said.

"Then why are you in a hurry? You do seem rushed."

Susan looked at me with a sense of pride. I could tell she had been waiting for this conversation for quite some time, and she was happy with her timing. She almost looked like she wanted to pat herself on the back.

"Why wouldn't I be? My best friend has been through a rough few months, and I want to give her something to smile about, along with the smile she will have every day we get to plan the wedding. That's what I'm here for, to make her smile, and I can't wait, knowing how excited she will get."

"Marriage is a big commitment. Can't you get her a dog or something?"

I felt a little bit puzzled. "I feel like you're trying to talk me out of this."

Susan hastily responded. "No, not at all. I just want you

to realize the commitment you're making."

"I do, I promise. It's a huge commitment, but at the same time, it's not a commitment at all. I can't wait to start a family and to wake up to her smile or for her to be there when I come home. People always see marriage as a big commitment, but if you've found the one you want to spend your future with, to me, all the day involves is getting up in front of your loved ones and expressing your love for each other."

I had paused for a second, smiling from ear to ear. "Nothing makes me smile more than thinking about our big day. To look my best friend in the eyes and tell her how much I love her, how much she means to me, and I know nothing would mean more to her, too."

"I guess we better get back to shopping then," Susan said as she stood up.

We wandered around Melbourne for another few hours, shopping at every jeweller store we could find, but it started to feel like a hopeless cause. The only rings that matched the description were too expensive. We called it a day and walked to the car.

"Are you okay?" Susan asked.

"Yeah, I guess."

"What's up?" Susan asked.

"I just thought I could get a nice ring, but I can't find any."

Susan looked at me. "You know it's the thought that counts."

There was silence.

"You know that, don't you?" she asked.

"Yeah, I know. Doesn't mean I didn't want to get her a nice ring to look at."

We drove home. Susan listened to her music, and I sat in silence. I was heartbroken, I had my heart set on a certain ring, and it didn't seem possible anymore.

"Are you okay?" she asked.

I shrugged, I had a fake smile for a moment.

"We will try again next week."

"Yeah, but where though?" I asked.

"Anywhere," she replied.

"If the city didn't have it, I doubt anywhere else will."

"Don't lose hope yet, Brendan. You'll find the ring, I promise. Now did you want to stop in town?"

"Only if that's okay. I need a bike lock."

We hopped out of the car and walked through the mall.

"Don't you want to look at jeweler shops why you're here?" Susan asked.

I shrugged, "I guess."

I had a browse at a jeweler window. There was the perfect ring, in fact, there were three of them. All the same design, yet different sizes. I was immediately attracted to the biggest one. Who wouldn't be? The only problem was I immediately fell in love. White gold band with three diamonds and a light blue center stone. We walked into the store.

The lady greeted us with a friendly smile. Her name badge said, Tiffany. "Welcome, how may I help you today?"

"Hey, there!" I said with enthusiasm. "We wanted to see the triple stoned light blue bands in the window over there." I pointed to the window where they were located. Tiffany walked us over and grabbed all three rings. She sat us down at the bench.

"Which one takes your fancy?"

I pointed to the biggest one.

"Ahh, of course," she said as she picked it up.

Susan and I examined the ring, I put it on my pinkie.

"What are you thinking?" Tiffany asked.

"I hope it's in my price range because there's a significant drop in size with the other rings."

Tiffany laughed. "It's Thirteen-thousand-five-hundred dollars."

I placed the ring back on the counter. I picked up the one next to it. "How much for this one?"

"Five thousand," Tiffany said with a questionable look on her face.

"The bigger one is over what I wanted to spend," I said as I handed back the ring. "Have you got any more rings of the same design? I don't know why I asked, it was a rare design to find.

"No, sorry, we don't, but you could try our sister store across the road."

My body filled with hope again. "Thank you for your help."

"No worries. Enjoy the rest of your day."

We immediately left the store and walked across the road.

"We only have fifteen minutes," Susan said.

"Don't worry. We know what we're looking for."

We followed the trail of windows around the outside of the shop. There were plenty of rings to decide from. Gold bands, silver bands, white diamonds, color diamonds. It took a while, but we finally reached the light blue diamond rings. A gentleman approached us.

"May I help you with anything?" he asked.

"Those rings there." I pointed to the blue ones. They were stacked on a tower, one above another. "How much for the top one?"

"Follow me inside the store, and we'll find out."

We walked into the store.

"It's Cam, by the way." Cam stretched out his hand to shake mine.

"I'm Brendan, and this is Susan." I gestured to my right.

Cam was mid-thirties, tall imposing stature with a glorious moustahce. He leaned into the case and grabbed the tower. We took a seat at the stools by the counter.

"Which ring were you looking at?" he asked.

"That one." I pointed to the top of the tower.

He grabbed the ring and handed it to me. "Very nice ring, and only eight thousand."

I looked at the ring. It was perfect, a white gold band with diamonds, triple stone setting with a light blue diamond in the middle. The perfect ring for the perfect girl. I handed the ring to Susan.

"Do you like it?" she asked.

"It's perfect." My body oozed with excitement. I could not contain my smile.

"Can you afford it?" she asked.

I shrugged and tilted my shoulders. "I guess I'll have to make it work."

Cam stayed there the whole time but was silent until then. He hadn't wanted to alter our decision in any way. "What's your price range?"

"I wanted to keep it under seven as a max," I responded.

Cam looked at his watch. "For about seven more minutes, it's thirty percent off. I'll go find a calculator."

I jumped up. "No need. It's fifty-six hundred, and you've got yourself a sale."

"Congratulations," he said with an outstretched arm. I shook his hand.

When Cam left to gather the paperwork, Susan asked. "Are you sure you want to do this?"

"Never been so certain in my life." I had the biggest grin on my face.

Susan gave me a big hug. "This is so exciting!"

"She still has to say yes," I cheekily added.

"As if she would say no," she responded with a glare.

Cam had returned with the paperwork. "Will you be paying in full today?"

"I can't withdraw that much on my card," I replied.

"It's no worries at all. You have twelve months to make payments. We just keep the ring stored in this safe until you make the final one. Would you like one last look at the ring?"

I nodded. It was everything I was searching for. I knew she would love it. I sure did. I handed the ring back to Cam, and he placed it in the safe. I filled out the paperwork, we shook hands, and Susan and I exited the store.

"I'm so excited," Susan said. "It's going to be hard to act normal. How do you contain it?"

I laughed and shook my head. "I have no idea."

"Where now?" Susan asked.

"I still need that bike lock." We both smiled and made our way to the bike store.

CHAPTER TEN: AN AMAZING HUNT

A liyah's birthday came fast. I was distracted by the ring and forgot to find the time to get her a good present. I had to make her day special in some way, instead. She'd spent the whole day at work. I was excited to see her when she finally came home.

"Welcome home." I wrapped her up in my arms, knowing the long stressful day she just had. "How was work?" I asked.

"Long, tiring, boring," she responded. "I just want to lay in bed and relax."

She kicked off her shoes off, walked towards the bed, but just as she went to collapse on the bed, she noticed the first letter.

Your clues can be found for each object. Each clue contains a letter. Put the letters together to complete a series of riddles and solve the puzzle for your present. Good luck! Your first riddle is primarily used for transport, but in this case, the object is stationary and used for weight loss.

With the most puzzled look on her face, Aliyah stared at me. "I'm not in the mood. Can't I just have my present now?" she asked.

"No," I responded. "It'll be fun trust me."

Unwillingly Aliyah began to think out loud, "Used for transport ... stationary ... is it the exercise bike?" She glanced at me, waiting to be proud of herself in hopes she was correct.

"You will have to go find out."

I followed Aliyah upstairs to where we kept the exercise equipment. She slowly warmed to the idea as she picked up the note.

"Ooooohhh, Ooooohhhh, I got it! I got it!"

Congratulations on finding the first clue. The letter required to solve the puzzle is D. Your next riddle is you could call me a key, play me at different pitches for a symphony.

"Well . . . What?" Aliyah looked confused as ever, "Is this one serious?"

I giggled a little bit. "Yeah come on, think! What is it?"

"I've got no idea," replied Aliyah. "Any hints?"

Shaking my head, I told her, "These are the easy ones. Symphony, what creates a symphony?"

"Instruments?" Aliyah still had a frown on her face as if the clue didn't help in any form of the manner. "Ahhhhh," she sighed. "The piano."

Aliyah made her way back downstairs to the piano to find the next note.

Your second letter is A. Your next riddle is round and round on cars I go, but please don't hang me down too low.

She turned and stared straight at me. "What the hell? Are you serious right now?"

"I really didn't think they were that hard, babe. What do we have on our property that also goes on a car?" I asked.

She just stared at me waiting for an answer.

"It can also be in our backyard. Don't hang me too—"

Before I could finish my sentence, Aliyah ran from the room straight out the backdoor, straight to the tire swing where she found the next note.

Next letter for the puzzle is T. Voyage around the world I must and to my _ _ _ _ _ _ _ do I trust.

Aliyah raced past me and straight upstairs, finally understanding the clues and a smile crept across her face. I followed her swiftly upstairs to the study to see her looking at our world map on the wall above the desk. Her smile immediately turned to sadness when she didn't see a note.

"I thought I figured one out by myself," she cried.

"Cough, check the back, cough" I tried to make it subtle, but it didn't work.

She searched behind the world map to find another note. Before reading it, she smiled at me. "You're an idiot, but thank you."

"Read it," I said, grinning from ear to ear.

Aliyah read aloud but muttered softly under her breath. *"The next letter to the puzzle is E, originally used for cooking food, now used for an entertainment mood.* You're killing me. Please tell me these get easier, Brendan."

"Ha-ha yeah, nah, I honestly thought this was easy." I smiled at her as I scrunched up my nose. "Come on, babe. Think! What do you use to cook?"

"An oven!" Aliyah's excitement was slowly changed when she saw the look on my face, "A Microwave?" There was no confidence in her answer.

"I was looking for heat for the answer, babe."

"Ohhh," she giggled. "A stove!"

Before I could stop her, she rushed to the kitchen. I trailed her as fast as I could.

"Where is it?" she asked.

"Read the second part of this riddle."

Aliyah muttered to herself. "Originally used for cooking food, now used for entertainment mood."

Aliyah held the paper close to her chest before looking up

at the roof, before she stared directly at me and rolled her eyes. "Firepit, isn't it?"

"I don't know, is it?" I replied.

Aliyah slowly made her way outside to find a piece of paper.

Your next letter for the puzzle is O. I'm only used to tell the time. I'm stuck on bloody half past nine.

Aliyah smiled and darted back inside to check the clocks. She walked past the kitchen, but the oven said 15:28. She then wandered into the lounge room to find a small clock on the mantelpiece, not ticking but reading nine-thirty. She peeled the piece of paper stuck to the back of the clock and mumbled to herself.

"My next letter is F, People claim a flower could never signify love."

Aliyah bolted out the front to the rose bushes, it was becoming hard to even keep up with her at that rate. By the time I got there, she was running around looking under and in the rose bushes, searching for her clue.

"Brendan, where is it? If you're thinking trees signify love again, I wouldn't even know where to start."

I began to chuckle. "Not this time but your roses never had to be outside."

Aliyah stared at me, "But there's no roses insi—Oh."

Aliyah wandered inside to her dresser to find blossoming white and green roses in a vase. "Brendan, I love them!"

"I didn't want to do the typical red roses, so I got white and green to match our room."

"They're amazing. I can trim them and put them in glasses and hang them from the windows."

It was nice to see her happy. That's all anyone deserves on their birthday.

"I just want to lay down and relax now. It's been a long

day. I really love the amazing race you've done, but is there much left? Can you just tell me the puzzle?"

"I knew it had been a long day for you. I'm so sorry. The code to my iPad is the date of our first kiss."

Puzzled but excited, Aliyah looked at me. "Firstly, never apologize for doing something so sweet. I am the one who is sorry for not having the energy. Secondly, where is the iPad?"

I handed Aliyah the iPad.

"You changed the background. Aren't I good enough to be your background?"

I smiled. "Stop being a gaggle and open the damn thing."

Aliyah mumbled to herself again. "Two-six-zero-three. Lucky that worked. I was worried I had the wrong date."

The iPad opened to a voucher for one free weekend away. She didn't get to choose the destination or the weekend. I planned to use it to propose.

CHAPTER ELEVEN: THE PERFECT VIEW

I made my payments on the ring over the next few months before the day came to propose. Aliyah had worked nice and early, so it was easy to plan the whole weekend. She was getting ready at her dresser.

"Are you still right to go away this weekend?" I asked.

Aliyah turned to face me. "Of course," she said excitedly.

I played my sad puppy card just to ensure she wanted to. I shrugged, tilted my head, and shoulders down, lowered my voice. "It's only going to be me and you, though."

Aliyah walked over and placed both hands on my cheeks. She lifted my head and kissed me on the lips.

"Don't be a goose," she whispered while staring into my eyes. "There's no place I'd rather be."

I couldn't contain my smile. It was such a nice feeling to be loved.

Aliyah smiled and kissed me on the forehead. "I have to go. Are you sure you're okay to pack everything? Are we leaving as soon as I get home from work?"

I nodded. "We will leave almost immediately if that's okay?"

"Of course, babe, I love you. Have a good day."

"You, too, beautiful." I managed to get those last words out as she walked out the door.

I ran back to our bedroom window and peered through the curtains just to be sure the car took off. After seeing Aliyah drive away, I grabbed my keys and headed for the front door. Susan ran out of her room and hugged me.

"Are you excited?" she asked.

"Today's the day." I didn't say anything else. I didn't want her to know about the roller coaster of emotions running through my head.

"Today is the day," Susan stated, putting a lot of emphasis on is. She took a step back and placed both her hands on my shoulders. "I'd wish you good luck, but you won't need it."

"Thank you," I said walking out the door.

I drove down to the jeweler to make my final payment on the ring. As I walked through the front doors, I was immediately greeted by Cam. At five past nine, I was the only customer. I had seen been in six or seven times to make the payments.

"Big fella." He greeted me straight away by shaking my hand. He was very cheerful. "How are you traveling?" he asked.

I shrugged. "Can't complain."

"Well?" he asked.

"It's today," I said.

Cam shook my hand again, his face lit right up. "Congratulations."

I could tell his excitement was genuine. "Thanks, mate," I replied.

"I'll go fetch your ring for you."

I followed Cam over to the safe. We made the final payment at the register, and Cam handed me some paperwork to sign. I lifted my head from the pages to see the ring in front of me.

"Now," Cam told me, "this red tub in front of me cleans the ring. It makes it very sparkly. However, do not leave it in the for longer than thirty seconds as it can erode the ring. We had a lady once who left it in there thinking the longer she left it, the cleaner it would become. Walked away and came back five minutes later to a black ring as the chemicals eroded the white gold plating."

"So no longer than thirty seconds?" I asked.

"Thirty seconds at the absolute most." Cam paused before adding, "Try not to do it more than every three months."

"Got it."

"Good luck, mate," Cam said, "I hope she loves whatever you have planned."

I walked out the shop and grabbed a few supplies before heading home for the day. I can't begin to describe to you how long that day went. I was too excited. I had finished packing by midday, and those last two hours waiting for Aliyah to come home seemed to take forever. Finally, I heard the front door open. I ran to greet Aliyah, wrapping her up in my arms. I kissed her on the forehead.

"How was your day?" I asked.

"Long . . . I'm tired," she said as she sunk into my arms.

"No. You can sleep on the drive down there. Do you need to pack anything or are you right to go?" I asked.

"Give me a better cuddle and five minutes."

She smiled as she said that, I gave her the tightest hug she had ever felt. She winced a little, and all the air escaped from her lungs. I even heard a back crack or two.

"All right, all right," she said, pushing me on the chest to get me away from her. "You win. I'll go get ready."

Aliyah changed quickly. We made our way to our week-end away.

"Where are we going?" she asked.

"That'd be a surprise."

"Get your cheeky grin off your face, babe. Where are we going?"

"Remember the place we stayed for our six-month anniversary?"

"Yes!" Aliyah had the biggest look of excitement in her

eyes. She slapped me on the arm. "I love that place so much. I love you so much. We can have roasted marshmallows by the fireplace and watched the sunset over the water. Oh my, I'm so excited."

"Why? I was just changing the topic. That's not where we're going."

Aliyah frowned and sunk back in her seat. The excitement from her voice had completely dispersed.

"You're actually an asshole." She did not hold back nor did she take jokes very well. "Why would you get me excited like that if we aren't going there?"

"Because we are going there."

Aliyah looked at me with a death stare. "I'm not even getting excited this time, don't even start.

"But we are." I had a cheeky laugh going. Aliyah's death stare became even more intense. "How about you use your teleporter and be surprised when we get there?"

Aliyah huffed and puffed and rolled over to face the window. "Get stuffed."

We had given the teleporter name to Aliyah because she always fell asleep during car rides. It was like a teleporter because these naps would last up to three hours at times.

I parked the car and gently shook Aliyah. "Beautiful, we're here!" I was excited, the only one at this stage. She woke from her slumber, slowly rubbing her eyes.

"Oh, my God, oh, my God! You said we weren't coming here. You . . . you . . ." She stopped for a moment. "Thank you!" She had a huge smile on her face.

"Shall we go inside?" I asked.

We did just that, I carried the luggage while Aliyah ran in.

"Did you bring the marshmallows?" she asked. I nodded. "You're the best," she said as she danced around the fireplace.

I was still standing at the front door taking it all in. It was nice to see her so happy.

"Oh, and the balcony," she said, unlocking the door and stepping outside.

Everything was the same. Same place, same furniture, same view, but the feeling was so much different. Last time was about discovering each other, our first holiday away. This time it felt right. Aliyah was enjoying a weekend away, and she should. She'd earned it. I, however, was taking in every second for what it was. The frames on the wall, the warm sea breeze on my face, the partial view I could see from where I was standing. Most importantly, her smile, the smile of the most perfect person I know.

Aliyah grabbed my arm. "What are you doing?"

"Seriously, come look at this."

I dropped the bags I was carrying, and Aliyah led me to the balcony. "Look," she said.

I didn't say anything, I just stood there. All you could see was the endless ocean of tree tops, and with that, the sun was setting over it.

Aliyah cuddled up under my arm and looked at me. "What are you thinking about?" she asked.

"Nothing."

"You're awfully quiet."

"What do you want for dinner? I'm starving."

Aliyah gazed out over the ocean. "I don't want to relive an old date."

"But?" I asked.

"But fish-n-chips with this sunset would be magical."

My ears pricked up when she said magical. She was right. "Then let's do it," I said.

"Are you sure?"

"I'm sure. It won't be reliving an old date. Let's make a new memory."

Aliyah smiled from ear to ear. "I'll go call the shop. Just fish and chips?"

"And a few dim sims, too, if that's all right."

"Of course," she said as she walked back inside to find her phone.

We drove down to the town to pick up dinner. Aliyah raced out of the car when we returned. "You take dinner to the balcony, I'll grab some cutlery and drinks."

I walked around the side of the house while Aliyah plodded around inside. We set up dinner and sat down on the floor. My eyes were focused on Aliyah while she gazed upon the view.

"Beautiful, isn't it?" she asked. Her concentration did not break, not once.

"Like you wouldn't believe," I replied. I never took my gaze off her. Moments are only as good as the people in them, and I was savoring every second. "What's the future?" I asked.

"What do you mean?"

"What are your plans? Do you see me in them?"

Aliyah turned to face me. "My plans are you, nothing but you. I'm nothing without you. I'd hope we could get married in the next five years, start a family together, you know? Go the distance, grow old together."

"Dance with me!" I jokingly demanded.

"Do you have music?"

I pulled my phone out of my pocket and pressed play, then took her in my arms.

Aliyah was looking up at me. "What are your plans, mister?" she asked.

I pulled away from her. "My plans?" I said touching my chest.

"Yes."

We had joined arms again and slowly swayed to the music.

"My plans? Well, my plans are you." I took a breath, and Aliyah smiled. Her head had found a new home, nestled tightly against my chest. "My plans are to be happy, and to be happy, my plans would have to be our plans."

"What would our plans be?" Aliyah asked.

"I don't really know, but I'd assume they'd involve maybe traveling for a bit, a house, some kids, growing old together."

"They're solid plans, I reckon, but you missed one."

"What's that?" I asked.

"The wedding in five years."

I was very nervous at that stage. I didn't understand why. I was confident in her response, but it was still too big a moment, and butterflies were having a party in my stomach.

"Why would we wait five years?" I hesitantly asked.

"What do you mean?" Aliyah asked.

I dropped to one knee.

Aliyah threw both of her hands to her face to cover her mouth. She teared up as she looked down at me. "This better not be a joke, like in the car."

I took both of Aliyah's hands. "Aliyah, I don't know much, but I know I've never been, nor will I ever be, as happy as I am when I'm with you. I don't want to picture a future without you because a future without you I hope will never exist. Aliyah, will you make me the happiest man on the planet?"

I reached into my back pocket and pulled out the box. I faced it toward Aliyah and opened it.

Aliyah had her hands on her face, wiping away tears. She nodded and presented her left hand for me to put the ring on. It was the perfect size, too. Her words were mumbled and broken. She rubbed her eyes again before helping me to my feet. I wrapped her up in my arms, and she placed her right ear on my chest and outstretched her left arm.

"It's so big and shiny! Are you sure you want to marry me?" she asked.

I held her tighter than I ever had before. "You're the most beautiful person I've ever met. Why wouldn't I want to spend the rest of my life with my best friend?"

Aliyah wiped her face again. "I'm just me. There's a whole world out there."

We swayed again. I whispered in Aliyah's ear. "You are my world."

We enjoyed another fifteen minutes out on the balcony. Our gentle sway had turned into a gentle dance.

"What now best friend?" I asked.

"I reckon we go inside and watch a movie."

We walked inside, Aliyah had her left arm stretched out in front of her the whole way, like a one-armed zombie.

"I still can't believe this. Do you mind if I call some people?"

"Of course not, beautiful."

While Aliyah was on the phone, I went to find the movies I'd bought down for the trip. Aliyah's phone began to ring. It was one of her oldest friends, Sia. Aliyah answered it and put it on the loud speaker.

"Are you actually serious right now?" Sia asked.

We both laughed.

I chimed in. "Well, hello to you too, Sia,"

"Hey, Brendan, but seriously, Aliyah, it's so shiny."

There were no breaks in her sentences. Sia was ecstatic, probably more than Aliyah, to be honest. I gave Aliyah a questionable look while she smiled.

"I sent her a photo." Aliyah said.

"Ahh," I said with a smile on my face. It was a nice feeling to see how happy she was.

"I can't wait to hear every little detail when you get back. For now, I'll let you guys enjoy your moment."

"I can't wait to show you the ring," Aliyah continued. "I love you."

"I love you, too, Sia," I added.

"I love you both so much. I'll speak to you soon."

Aliyah disconnected.

"Oh, I have another present for you," I said as I jumped out of bed.

"No, no more surprises. You've done more than enough tonight. I'll have a heart attack."

I handed Aliyah a wrapped parcel. "What is it?" She lifted the parcel to her ear and shook it. There was no noise. "No seriously, what is it?"

I shrugged. "You'll have to open it and find out."

Aliyah gently unwrapped the present. I never understood that. She liked to keep the wrapping paper intact rather than just ripping into it.

"Oh, wow. This will be handy," she said, holding the binder.

"I know," I responded. "I thought it would really help."

Aliyah turned through the pages. There was a checklist to help with the twelve months leading up to the wedding. Tabs marked a section for each of those checklist items, so we could source different venues and caterers, etc. You could easily keep them all on the same place and compare them.

"Thank you so much," Aliyah said hugging me.

"You don't need to thank me at all."

"No, I really do. You're so kind and thoughtful, thank you." Aliyah closed the binder and placed it on the floor next to the bed. "Do you mind if I call my parents?"

"Go for it."

I walked to the kitchen, poured myself a glass of water,

and leaned against the bench. The last few hours had been full on and exciting. I just needed a moment to collect my thoughts. After a few minutes, Aliyah surfaced from the room and cuddled up to me.

"What's my man up to?" she asked.

"How were your parents?" I asked.

"Ignore my question then." Aliyah glared angrily at me. but I could tell she was joking as she began laughing. "Nah, they're really good. They can't wait to see us." Aliyah took a sip from my water. "Are you coming back to bed?"

I followed Aliyah back into the room, and we snuggled up to watch the show.

I woke up smelling bacon and eggs the next morning.

"You didn't have to," I exclaimed as Aliyah bought the tray table into the room.

"What, this?" She raised the tray. "This is mine. You'll have to go cook your own."

I slumped and ripped the covers off me, only jokingly, of course.

"Get back into bed, you goose. This is a thank you."

"I don't need to be thanked."

"Last night was perfect. I really appreciate that you look at me the same way I look at you."

We finished our breakfast before packing our belongings and heading home. Both our families were waiting for us to have a big lunch and celebrate. Aliyah opened the car door and was immediately swamped as they ran to greet us.

"Show us the ring! Show us the ring!" a few of them cried.

Aliyah presented the ring to Mum, Susan, and Theresea.

"I love the blue diamond!" Mum said.

The rest was background noise though. Mum and Dad wrapped me up in their arms. "Congratulations, my boy," Mum said with tears in her eyes.

"We're proud of you," Dad whispered.

We all sat down and enjoyed a late lunch. Mum had whipped up a ripper of a roast to celebrate our engagement. The girls were all gathered around one end of the table. The wedding planning had already started. Dad and I had sat on the other side of the room.

"Are you nervous?" he asked.

"What for?" I asked back.

"Everything. Getting married, having kids. I mean you're only twenty, and hell, that shit still scares me at times."

"I'll be fine."

"Brendan, you've always been someone who worries. You've had your fair share of troubles, and you've always worried about the direction life's taking you. How can you be so sure?" Dad asked.

I turned to look at Aliyah, in between all the commotion and conversations in the room we managed to catch each other's gaze, we both smiled like little school kids.

"Because no matter what I do, Dad, nothing in life is more important to me than seeing her smile, I know everything will be okay as long as I can make her happy."

Dad patted me on the leg. "You're both happy, and that's all that matters to me."

Chapter Twelve: Foundations of a Future

I carried that comment with me for quite some time. Dad was right. I was happy. We both were. what else mattered? After months of planning and preparation, one of the big days had finally arrived, our engagement party. The backyard looked exquisite with fairy lights and lanterns hanging from a big tree in the courtyard. The beams we had running across the backyard for the grapevines were covered in lights with a beautiful crystal chandelier to complement the middle.

I was getting dressed in our room.

"Are you still not dressed yet?" Aliyah asked as she entered the room.

"I don't know what to wear," I joked with a smile on my face.

That smile turned into a cheeky grin as I stood in front of the mirror with my back to Aliyah. I had my grey suit in one hand, my black in another, and I was alternating each suit in front of my body.

"Which one?" Aliyah asked.

I began to speak as I turned around. "I really like the grey" I stopped mid-sentence, my focus fixed on Aliyah. She wore one of the most stunning white dresses I had ever seen.

"But?" she asked.

I smiled and didn't answer.

"What?" she asked again with her hands on her hips,

looking like she was short for time.

"Daaayyyuuuummm!" I exclaimed as I threw my suits on the bed. I walked to Aliyah and grabbed her by the waist. She was blushing and giggling and tried not to make eye contact.

"Is this the dress I wasn't allowed to see?" I asked.

Aliyah nodded. I took a step back and looked her up and down. I raised my arm and signaled for Aliyah to turn around. Aliyah grabbed the dress by the sides and pivoted swiftly before cheekily smiling at me.

"Slower!" I demanded.

Aliyah did a slower pivot.

"Babe," I exclaimed, "that low back, those back muscles."

Aliyah completed her turn, as I pulled her close to me with my hands on her hips. "Thank you for the surprise. You look so beautiful!"

"You're just saying that," Aliyah said bowing her head to the floor.

"No, I'm serious. I'm worried with you looking like that you're going to leave this party with another fiancé."

Aliyah shook her head from side to side. "It'd be kind of weird, though. Most of them are my family."

I was about to interrupt when she laughed. I loved her laugh. I loved her smile, and besides, she called my bluff and made me smile.

"I really love you," I said as I kissed her.

"I'll always love you more." Aliyah slapped me on the chest twice. "Your guests have started to arrive. Just put on a bloody suit."

"I don't know what to wear."

"Which one do you like better?" she asked.

With no hesitation, I answered, "Grey."

"But?"

"I don't want to wear a jacket. Just the sleeves rolled up

and tie kind of look."

"Why can't you wear the grey then?"

"Because the black matches the black tie."

"Don't care. Grey it is. Just put it on and let's go!"

By the time I finished ironing my shirt, got dressed, and headed outside, there were at least twenty guests in the backyard. It was February, so so even at seven-thirty, there was still plenty of sunshine left. The sun began to set, filling the sky with a beautiful orange glow.

"About time!" my dad snarled as he walked over to me with his arms wide open.

"Yeah, seriously, who the hell is late to their own party?" Theresea asked.

Dad gave me a hug, shortly followed by a kiss on the cheek by my sister. My mum closely followed them and engulfed herself in my arms.

"You look amazing, Mum!" I said.

"Thank you. As do you!"

"Have you seen Aliyah's dress?" I asked.

"Of course, she always steals the show, doesn't she? I can't wait to see her wedding dress.

"She's the most stunning bride to be," my sister added.

Theresea had never been close with my brother or his girlfriends, but she adored Aliyah. Theresea consistently told us on a constant basis to never let go, as neither one of us was ever going to do better.

"You want a beer?" Dad asked.

I looked at Dad, and he looked back at me. "Oh, right, what girl drink do you want tonight?"

"I'm not sure. Just make it sugar-free."

"We'll go get you a drink so you can say hello to the rest of your guests."

"Thanks, guys. I love you all."

"Love you, too," they all said, walking off.

We had a gazebo down at the side of the house, and it was beautiful, filled with flowers and fairy lights strung from side to side. It served as an entrance to the party. and as much as it took a long time to set up, I must admit it was worth it. I stood by the end of the gazebo and the start of the backyard, greeting all our guests as they arrived. That went on for an hour, catching up with everyone for a few minutes before they would leave me for the next arrival. Finally, my mates showed up.

"Look at ya, snazzy pants!" Jackson laughed.

"You look so pretty," Kieran added while patting my head.

Aaron and Jake followed. We participated in our group handshakes and hugs.

"I still can't believe you're getting married. You're the youngest of us by a nautical mile." Aaron finished our handshake with a hug. "I'm proud of you, mate."

"Thanks, buddy," I responded as we parted

"You guys ready for a mammoth occasion? I have to do some more greets, but after that, I'm coming for you. Beers are down the back."

"We will catch you soon," Tom said as they wandered off.

I was immediately hugged from behind, although it felt like a tackle. Aliyah had her arms around my waist and was peeking her head from around my side. I turned to face her.

"How's my beautiful boy?" she asked.

"I'm doing swell. How's my angel?"

Aliyah shrugged but then smiled.

"How many have you had, you cheeky little devil?" I asked.

Aliyah shrugged and smiled again.

I giggled. "I love you."

Aliyah shook her head. "You know I'll always love you more."

The night had been a blast. Everyone gathered around the steps for speeches. There stood Dad, Aliyah, Trevor, and myself in front of a crowd, approximately two hundred people.

Dad began, "Hey, everyone, good evening. I'm the father of the groom, and this is my counterpart." Dad patted Trevor on the back. "You're up, big fella."

Dad pushed Trevor forward. Trevor stumbled a little bit, then wiped his forehead. "Uhh-uhh," he stuttered. "I wasn't aware I was going to make a speech. Ah . . . I'm certainly not good a public speaking at the best of times." Trevor turned to face me.

"Want me take over?" I whispered. Trevor nodded and took a step back.

"Hey all, future male bride here." A little snicker came from the crowd, not much though. "All I wanted to say is a huge thank you to everyone for coming out and making this day so special. Your support and kind wishes are definitely appreciated."

I turned to face Aliyah and stretched out my hand. She stretched hers out to meet mine.

"We're really excited to begin our journey together, and we really appreciate everyone for showing up to help us celebrate. Last, but not least, I want to thank Mum and Susan for their behind the scenes work in the kitchen and anyone else who has helped out in that respect."

Dad stepped forward next to Aliyah and me. "That was a fun lot of speeches. I do want to say one more thing before everyone parts ways."

Dad turned to face Aliyah and I and smiled. He raised his glass of champagne.

"To two people who mean the absolute world to me. Anyone who has spent a minute in your presence knows that you've found what most people spend their whole life looking for. I know plenty of couples who have been married twenty years and have never experienced love like you two."

Everyone went dead silent. You could easily have heard a pin drop.

"Millions of planets, billions of people. I'm just so glad you two found each other."

Dad went silent. You could hear all the emotion in his voice as he was speaking so he must have truly meant it.

Trevor raised his glass. "To Aliyah and Brendan."

Everyone joined in. "To Aliyah and Brendan."

Mum and Susan immediately started serving cake. Dad came up and hugged me.

Still embracing, I asked, "You all right?"

"You deserve all the happiness in the world after what you've been through. Don't let go of her, all right?"

"Thanks, Dad. I won't."

The next hour consisted of saying goodbye to everyone that was leaving. By eleven o'clock there were only thirty people left, all our close friends and relatives. Aliyah and her best friends were gathered around the fire pit while I began cleaning up.

"You got a pigskin?" I heard from behind me. It was Aaron.

I turned around. "Of course, I do."

He followed me to my room where we grabbed the football and headed out to the street. The rest of the boys followed with plenty of drinks. Aaron threw the ball to Jackson, who ran off celebrating.

"Reggie Wayne in the end zone!" He ran away with both hands in the air—one had the football, and the other had a beer.

"Are we about to?" Aaron cut me off.

"Yeah, Brendan, street gridiron."

"Aww, yeah," Tom said followed by a laugh.

"Aww, yeah," I chimed in with. "Who's starting quarterback?"

"The wife bride," Jackson said as he handed me the football.

Everyone laughed. "Wife bride?" I asked.

"Bloody hell, Jackson." Tom hit Jackson across the back of the head.

"Well, what is it?" Jackson asked.

"It was male bride, you dickhead," Tom replied.

Jackson nodded. "Well, all right. Can we just play?"

The game didn't last very long at all. There was a lot of stumbling and very few catches.

"One last play," Jake begged.

We all shrugged. "Yeah, all right," we agreed.

Aaron, Jackson, and I all huddled. "What are we running, wife bride?" Jackson asked.

"Just leg it," I answered. We lined up. "Red eighty-nine, red fourteen, red twenty-six, hut, hike, hike!"

I stood up, arms outstretched in the air. Jackson was still crouched in front of me. "What the hell man?" I asked.

"What?" Jackson asked.

"Hike the ball, mate."

"Oh, yeah, well fair enough, aye."

He stood up and threw the ball at my chest before running away. I threw the deep ball to Aaron, who tripped on the bitumen. Jake ran around, waving his hand in the air.

"Denied." He started wiggling his index finger. "Peyton Manning denied you."

"Peyton Manning is a quarterback, you idiot." Tom agreed with Aaron.

"Yeah and that," he said, wiggling his index finger, "is Dikembe Mutumbo, who played basketball."

"Do you even watch sports?" Jackson asked.

We sat down in the gutter to finish our beers.

"Thanks for coming tonight, fellas."

"It was our pleasure, mate. Thanks for having us." Jackson remarked as he finished his beer.

"Are you nervous?" Aaron asked.

"Not yet," I said with a laugh.

Aaron shook his head shook his head. "I still don't get that," he said with a questioning look as he continued. "All of us are older and have been with our girls for seven, eight, nine years. Not one of us is engaged. You're twenty and ready to start having kids. I just don't get it."

"Yeah, I don't understand it, either, but I'm bloody happy for ya, mate," Tom said patting me on my leg as he stood up.

"I'm going to call a taxi. Are you coming with us to town?" Tom asked.

"Nah, I'm going to stay here. Thanks, though." I replied.

People emerged from the house as the taxis arrived. It was Aliyah's friends, and they were going out on the town. I had said my thank you and goodbyes before heading inside. Aliyah was curled up in the corner of the dining room, fast asleep.

"Hey," I said gently shaking her, "are you okay?"

Aliyah opened her eyes for a split second. "It all caught up with me in the end. I'm so tired!"

"You poor thing. Let's get you to bed." I lifted Aliyah up to her feet, and we walked slowly to the bedroom. We passed my parents and hers along the way.

"Aww, the poor thing," Mum said.

"Yeah, she will sleep well. Thank you for everything tonight. We truly appreciate it. We love you guys."

"We love you, too," Susan said as they all smiled.

I walked off and tucked Aliyah into bed.

CHAPTER THIRTEEN: TRADITIONALLY SPEAKING

Two months had passed, and it was Easter time, time to get chocolate drunk. Although we were technically adults, Easter only had two things, a big family dinner and the mother of all Easter egg hunts. That year though, due to conflicting schedules, we didn't wake up to an egg hunt, but a new tradition was born, a night hunt. The rules were simple. We each got one torch, and whoever collected the most eggs won. We all gathered in my room while the Easter bunny hid the eggs.

"Who is going to win this year?" Theresea asked us all.

"Could be Brendan. He's won the last three," Ben's girlfriend, Kim, replied.

Ben paced in the tiny room, two steps one way, two steps the other. We all watched him from the bed.

"Nah, I've got it this year. I've got a secret weapon." He had a sly look on his face. He had come prepared and pulled a little blue torch out of his pocket. It was bright enough.

"You see, it's strategic," he said pointing to Kim and Theresea's gigantic torches.

"I only have a small torch to mess around with while grabbing eggs." Ben turned to face Aliyah and me.

"What did you guys bring?" he asked.

We didn't say a word. We just turned to each other and grinned. We pulled out our torches, extended the bands, and fixed them firmly on our foreheads.

Aliyah laughed. "You see, it's strategic," she said.

"Ha-ha got him!" Theresea shouted at the top of her lungs. She jumped off the bed and moved towards Ben. "Good luck now."

The door behind us opened. Mum and Dad stepped in and closed the door behind them. Ben ran to them, but Mum stretched her arm out and put her palm in his face. "Wait!" she exclaimed.

"Now," Dad began. "You each get a bag to stash your eggs."

Mum hand out the bags. They were cute. Each bag had a different color and design. Somehow, I got the pink bag with a fluffy bunny on it.

Dad continued. "There's one hundred and thirty-five eggs placed around the house and in the garage. One torch per person. Good luck."

Dad stepped to the side and opened the door. We all leaped from our starting positions and raced out the door. It all happened so fast. Outside my room was the room with the pool table and the bar, a haven for Easter eggs. Ben, Kim, and Theresea were all fighting for eggs, so Aliyah and I ran straight downstairs. She took the theatre room while I took the guest bedroom. We both gathered roughly ten eggs before meeting in the hallway.

A ruckus was still going on upstairs. Before they moved downstairs toward us, we ran down the hall to the living area. Aliyah went left to the couch and TV while I went right to the kitchen. We were being closely followed. Our Easter hunts were always exhilarating, but the whole no lights rule took it to another level.

There was plenty of panic. Theresea ran past me, through the laundry and into the garage. Ben was fighting with Aliyah for any eggs they could find while Kim ran to join me in the kitchen. She was about two meters from me when she looked at the laundry door. She took a few steps before turning back to face me. She took a few quick steps before turning and running through the laundry to the garage. I found a fair few eggs within the kitchen before Kim and Theresea came back from the garage and sat at the dinner table.

"Finished, are we?" Mum asked.

"I reckon so," Theresea responded.

Aliyah, Ben, and I joined them at the table. We began counting our eggs. Mum turned the lights on so we could see.

"What did you get?" Theresea asked Aliyah.

Aliyah put her hand up to signal for Theresea to hold on a sec. "Thirty-six, thirty-seven," she mumbled to herself. "I got thirty-eight, eggs. You?"

"Twenty-three," Theresea replied.

"Bit light on eggs, sis," I said and snickered.

"What did you get?" She replied.

"I haven't finished counting yet." I went back to counting my eggs.

"Okay, what did everyone get?" Mum asked.

We went in a counterclockwise direction.

"Twenty-four," Ben said.

Kim followed. "Nineteen."

"Twenty-three," Theresea added.

"Thirty-one," I said, smiling.

"I guess our winner is Aliyah with thirty-eight," Mum said and cheered.

"Looks like you've been dethroned," Dad laughed as he punched me in the arm.

Aliyah hit me on the other arm. "Not the king anymore?"

"Aye, hold up, Congrats," I said. I was smiling but I was a little bit pissy. Winning the egg hunt held a lot of merit in our household.

"What's one hundred and thirty-five divided by five?"

Aliyah asked.

"Twenty-seven, babe" I responded.

Aliyah pulled out eleven Easter eggs and put them on the table while I added four.

"All done," she smiled.

"You ready?" I called from the stairs. It was my resident seating spot while Aliyah always took forever to get ready.

She emerged from our room in a white jumpsuit and white heels.

"You look stunning." I smiled as I pulled her closer by the hips for a kiss.

"As do you," she replied, running her hands down my chest. We were both wearing white, complete white. There was a festival in Melbourne, and I wasn't sure what it was or the meaning behind it. It was our first time going. All I knew was you had to wear white, and the festival went from sunset to sunrise. We enjoyed a nice car ride up, but parking was a pain. We ended up parking six blocks away and walking down. As we slowly strolled toward the event, people's clothes changed from every colour to white, music appeared in the distance, and shops showed decorations for the event.

"This is so exciting!" Aliyah shouted, although it really sounded like a whisper as the music and crowd kept getting louder. We dawdled through the crowd. Aliyah had both hands wrapped around my left arm. It was a very tight squeeze as she didn't want to get lost in the crowd. Markets and food stalls were everywhere. There was plenty of live entertainment, and with all of that on a beautiful night out on the river, came plenty of people dressed in white.

"Wow!" Aliyah exclaimed.

"What?" I asked.

"I've always seen these posts on social media about all white this and all white that. We could have an all-white wedding. It would look so elegant."

"Yeah, except for the fact I won't look good in a white suit."

Aliyah rested her hand on my shoulder. "You'd pull it off better than you would realize."

We sat down by the stage, eating sushi and watching the performers. It was such a gorgeous night for that time of the year. We watched break dancing and a lot of singing.

"It might be time to make a move," I said.

"Already?" Aliyah asked with a tone of disappointment.

"It has been two hours. Time really did fly."

We got up and began to walk back to the car.

"I reckon if we come back next year, we will be able to book a hotel and spend the whole night here."

Aliyah smiled and tightened her grip on my arm. "I'd love that."

We had to leave early to make the two-hour drive to where we were staying in the mountains for the night. Both Aliyah's and my parents were at another festival, watching a heap of bands. It'd been a long day for them with lots of alcohol, so we were picking them up. Driving through Melbourne was tough enough, especially on a night where half the streets were closed off.

Our turn off came up fast. Once we finally got out of the city, we could relax a little bit and listen to some music. While we were there, Aliyah wanted to look at wedding venues nearby. We were excited to start shopping around. We had two in mind that were farther away, so we bookmarked them for the later the next day.

We arrived at the festival to a long line of cars going through the pick-up bay. Eventually, we got to the front and parked. We hopped out of the car to greet our parents before splitting up and saying our goodbyes.

I held Aliyah very tight. "Are you sure you're okay to

drive my car?" I asked.

Aliyah nodded. She was never comfortable driving other people's cars, especially when they were worth a little bit. Also, Aliyah was shocking with direction. Just picture having a GPS that doesn't know left from right or thinks one-hundred meters is actually five-hundred meters.

"Are you going to follow me or the GPS?" I asked.

"The GPS," she responded.

"I love you. Drive safe." I gave Aliyah a kiss as she got into the car.

"I love you, too. I'll call if I need you." Aliyah drove off with Mum and Susan in the car.

Dad, Trevor, and I waved as they drove off.

"Where are we parked?" I asked.

"This way." Dad gestured as we turned and began to walk.

The festival had been held on a big property. It took us almost fifteen minutes to walk across it to get to the other car park. They had some brilliant stories though to keep us entertained for that walk.

We were staying at a brand-new hotel they had just built to accommodate all the skiers for snow season. I dialed Aliyah's phone.

"You're here already?" she asked.

"Yeah," I responded. "Where are you?"

"Room 481. Follow the corridor all the way to the end, then turn left."

We did just that. I spend the five-minute walk trying to keep Dad and Trevor silent so they wouldn't wake the other guests at one in the morning.

Dad thumped the door with a closed fist. Susan opened it.

"Hello, family!" Dad yelled at the top of his voice as he walked in. He had his arms raised and wide open almost like he was waiting for a hug.

"How'd you get here so fast?" Mum asked.

"We had a race car driver," Trevor responded.

"Yeah, I was feeling a bit ill," Dad told them. "But for some reason the car didn't make me feel worse." Dad turned to face me. "How'd you manage that?"

"Manage what?" I asked.

"To drive so fast yet so smooth around all those corners. That road was not straight at any stage. You read them beautifully."

Everyone turned to face me after Dad's question.

"He drives with both feet," Aliyah said. "He has one on the brake and one on the accelerator. Very good at it, too."

"That explains a lot. You can ease onto the brake rather than switching pedals and jerking," said Trevor.

I just nodded.

"Who wants another drink?" Mum shouted. I don't think she meant to shout, but she just wasn't aware of how loud she was. She stood up from the end of the bed and walked over to the bar fridge.

"You have a drinking problem, you alcoholic," Susan laughed.

"No. Alcoholics go to meetings. I go to parties," Mum responded.

"Spoken like a true alcoholic," Dad snickered.

"Shut up!" Mum snarled at Dad. She turned to face the room, holding a six pack of Johnny Walkers. "A drink anyone?"

"Nah, I think it's bedtime for me," Aliyah responded.

"Me, too, I guess then." I made my way around to give everyone a kiss goodnight, as did Aliyah. As we left, we heard a collective "Sleep tight" from all our parents.

"Don't stay up too late," I stated, pointing my finger at them.

The next day we all got ready, met to sit around at the restaurant table, and ordered our food. Mum, Susan, and Trevor all rested their heads on their arms with their elbows on the table. Dad was the odd, lively one—he sat there watching videos on his phone.

"Big night everyone?" I cheekily asked. Trevor grunted, Mum did nothing, and Susan lifted her head. "Shhhh," she added with her finger over her lips.

We ate our breakfast and began our car trip to the first wedding spot.

"I'm so excited!" Aliyah jumped up, almost out of her seat. I rested my hand on her leg. She held it.

"Me, too, beautiful."

Our first spot was an older country mansion. We arrived at the car park, which had a huge water fountain. The venue sat on a hill and doubled up as a restaurant and cafe during the day.

We were greeted by a lady. "Welcome! I'm Sharon. How may I help you today?"

"Pleased to meet you. We've come to look at this venue for a wedding."

"Brendan, is it?" She gestured toward me. I nodded. "This must be the lovely bride to be?" She walked over toward Aliyah. "May I see the ring?"

Aliyah stretched out her hand for Sharon. Sharon took Aliyah's hand and gazed upon the ring. "What a beautiful ring," she stated. Sharon turned her attention to Mum and Dad. "I'm assuming you're the parents?"

"Bill," Dad said.

"I'm Samantha," Mum said, touching her chest.

"Susan," Susan said, repeating Mum's motion.

"Trevor," Trevor stated, stepping forward.

"Come on in, guys. Let's go for a tour." Sharon led us

through the front doors to the dining hall. "This is where your reception would be. The main hall seats a hundred and twenty guests and can be set up in many arrangements."

The main hall was beautiful, limestone brick walls with wooden floorboards. All the furniture was wooden, too, even the bar.

Sharon gestured to the bar. "The bar is in the middle of the room against the back wall. It's a convenient central location for all guests to order from. We also have waiters to bring drinks to each guest. To our left here is a small room with a small table. That's just for the bride and groom to escape if they ever need. Down the end of the room is the big double doors which open to the dance floor."

"That's different, having two rooms for your reception and dance floor," Susan stated.

"Yes, we found a lot of guests wanted to sit and have a chat, but also get on the dance floor, so we built an extension to make it a little quieter in here. You'll be able to see properly as we walk around."

Sharon walked through the hall and led us to the outside. The doors were on the left side of the hall, opposite the bar. The whole wall was glass, to allow people to enjoy the view. We walked outside and down the steps.

"This is the terrace. I have to go help our staff quickly, so have a look around. I'll meet you back here in ten?"

"Certainly," I responded.

We all wandered around the terrace and surrounding property. Up the back behind the hall was a garden with a heap of old rusted farming equipment. It was nice and looked to be from the 1800s, just wasn't what we were after. We made our way back to the terrace. The terrace had three levels with stairs down the center. Each level had a break wall in them filled with a lovely array of flowers. The bottom level of the terrace overlooked the valley, and although it was gorgeous, it also wasn't. I stood next to Aliyah who was gazing out into the distance upon the valley. I held her hand.

"What do you think?" I asked.

"I like it, but I don't love it," she responded.

"Why?" I asked.

"Honestly, I have no idea, I just don't love it."

Aliyah turned to face me. I was still staring off into the distance.

"What do you think?" she asked.

I shrugged. "It's nice, but it's not it, definitely not it. I think it's the view."

I raised my hand to point. "Over there are beautiful pine trees and over there, there's beautiful green grass, but there are so many breaks in between of dead grass and cattle. Not really the scenic backdrop we're after."

Aliyah nodded. "Glad someone put a finger on it. Shall we head to the next one?"

I nodded.

Hand in hand with our parents following, we made our way back up the terrace steps. As we were about to step inside, Sharon greeted us at the door. "My apologies for that. Now, what did we think?"

"We really appreciate your time," I began. "It's a really beautiful establishment. It's just not what we're after."

Sharon shook all our hands. "It was a pleasure meeting you all. I wish you the very best with your big day."

Sharon walked back inside while we walked around the side to our cars.

"Where to next?" Trevor asked.

"Covent park," Aliyah responded.

After another hour and a half in the car, we arrived at our destination. It was beautiful. Covent Park, an establishment in the mountains, had an unimpeded view of the city. We stood on the edge of the balcony in awe of such a breath-taking view. Not only was the view of the city great, but the weather perfectly complimented it with an overcast day and a heap of clouding around. There must have been a huge gap right on the skyscrapers, as beams of light broke through the clouds, giving the city a beautiful light.

We walked up the stairs and found someone.

"Well, hello there," he said smiling. "How may I help you?"

"We're here to see Gregory," I responded.

"Guilty!" he exclaimed raising his right hand.

Gregory was someone I would love to have organize our big day. He was as flamboyant as they come, and you could already tell he took a lot of pride in his work.

"Are you Brendan?" he asked.

I nodded. "We spoke on the phone."

"Yes, we did, I'd love to show you around." He paused for a moment and changed his stance, one hand on his hip, and the other hand complimented his sentences. "Unfortunately, I've got a wedding on in half an hour, and the cake is an absolute disaster. The top two tiers are caving in." Gregory paused to wipe sweat from his forehead. "The Bon veneers didn't show up nor did the chair covers the bride said she was going to bring. I'm a little bit stressed."

We were all puzzled, but some days everything just goes wrong.

"Do you have any questions?" Gregory asked.

"Is the ceremony private? There seems to be a lot of people around," Aliyah asked.

I could see Aliyah was eager to ask the question, and I don't blame her in not wanting a lot of tourists wandering around on her special day.

"In here is private. You get your own personal balcony with spectacular views." Gregory gestured to the glass doors where the balcony connected. "As far as privacy goes though, it's a publicly owned facility so I don't like your chances. If you want your ceremony in the private gardens, there will be no unwanted guests, but we can't block off the rest of the garden for a ceremony."

Aliyah nodded.

"Any other questions?" Gregory asked.

There was silence.

"Well, have a look around. Please don't go into the private gardens until the ceremony is over. Oh, and come and find me before you go."

We shook hands. "Actually, mate, you look like you've got enough on your plate. I'll call you during the week. Good luck."

I turned and followed my family down the stairs, out the door, and into the gardens. There wasn't a person to be seen in there. I guess all the tourists come for the view or for a coffee at the cafe and didn't realize the gardens were down the back. To me, as much as the views were breathtaking, the gardens should have been the main attraction. The gardens were beautiful, peaceful, and so tranquil. The arrangement of flowers and fauna were complimented by the sound of trickling water from the many water features. We all explored the gardens before noticing the ceremony in the private gardens had ended. All that separated the private gardens from the reception hall was a little road, with a lot of people.

The bride and groom had to scrimmage through a crowd of people before boarding their chariot to leave the ceremony in a horse and carriage. Getting wedding photos must have been hard. Even once they were in the carriage, people were still trying to take photos with the horses. Some people just have no respect or courtesy. We waited for half an hour for all the guests to make their way into the reception hall before sneaking into the private garden. It wasn't exactly a garden, so to speak. There were tall hedges all the way around to gain some privacy, but on the inside, there wasn't much at all. Just a rotunda with chairs facing it on some lawn. No flowers or features, just grass and hedges.

I was standing about five meters in front of the rotunda when Aliyah came and hugged me from behind.

"What are you thinking, beautiful boy? It's not it, is it?" Aliyah asked.

I turned to face Aliyah. She had that look on her eyes that she wasn't a fan at all. I turned my head to face the parents, who were already jokingly playing out the ceremony in the rotunda.

"Pack her up, boys," I stated.

"Why?" Mum asked.

"Not it," I responded.

"Where to next?" Susan asked.

Aliyah and I looked at each other. "Home," Aliyah answered.

That's where we headed. Going back through the city was a breeze, for once. Four o'clock on a Sunday afternoon was certainly better than during the week. We were just leaving Melbourne when I received a phone call from my Mum.

"Yes'um," Aliyah answered.

"The four of us were just thinking. The lighthouse on the side of the highway overlooking the bay, have you considered it?"

"Nah, I can't say we have," Aliyah responded.

"What'd she say?" I asked.

Aliyah covered the bottom of the phone, so they couldn't hear us. "They suggested that lighthouse on the way home. What do you think?"

"I'm thinking let's go home look online and suss out a few more places tomorrow."

Aliyah nodded. "Maybe tomorrow," she said before hanging up the phone. "What are we going to do tonight?" Aliyah asked.

"I reckon let's get some dinner and research some places for tomorrow."

"I agree."

"Any ideas for dinner?" I asked.

"We haven't been to Lock-n-Ness in ages. Can we go there?"

"Of course!" I grabbed her hand.

We arrived at the pub and took the last table available. They had to clear the cutlery and plates from the last couple as we took our seats. Lock-n-Ness was in a small suburb outside of town, about a twenty-minute drive. It had a population of around two thousand. No one ever knew anyone from there. I doubt anyone could even tell you where the houses were, but on the side of the highway stood a pub, arguably one of the best and busiest. Everyone knew of the Lock-n-Pub for two reasons, the food and the music.

"Are you excited?" I asked.

"Of course."

"Not nervous at all?" I was asking the questions to try and get honest answers out of her.

"Just excited," she said smiling from ear to ear.

Aliyah reached over the table and grabbed my hand, rubbing my knuckles with her thumb.

"Nothing excites me more than knowing I get to spend the rest of my life with you. I just want to find the right place, so we can get to planning immediately." Aliyah paused for a moment. I could sense she was overjoyed. The tone in her voice had also changed. "I'm just so excited."

Our dinner arrived nice and quickly, and it lived up the expectations. We paid and then were on our way. It was only seven o'clock with a beautiful sunset in the distance.

"Let's make a quick detour," I said to Aliyah.

"Where to?"

"It's a surprise," I said, grinning.

We arrived at Stellar Hill Vineyards, just outside of the city. A long driveway honestly seemed a kilometer long. It was a little bit curved and took us through their decent sized vineyards to the car park beside the restaurant. As we drove past the house, we came across the peak of the hill and began to descend into the most stunning view.

"Wow." Aliyah gasped, clearly taken by the view just as much as I was. Nothing but grass fields stretched from horizon to horizon. The restaurant overlooked those beautiful fields, and off in the distance, behind them is where the sun would set.

"How'd you find the place?" Aliyah asked.

"I just had heard about the views so thought we could try it."

It was about a five-hundred-meter walk from the car park to the establishment. The restaurant also had outdoor seating on the terrace. We climbed the stairs and turned around for a moment to witness the sunset on the horizon. It was fields of grass with an unimpeded view of a sunset at its finest.

"Could you stand here and get married in front of that?" I asked.

Aliyah cradled herself in my arms and wrapped her arms around my waist. She didn't say a word. She just looked deeply into my eyes and nodded.

We hopped in the car and drove in silence for a good ten minutes. We made eye contact a few times but couldn't hold back our smiles. The wedding had become real. We drove out to Mum and Dad's after dinner, a Sunday night tradition. Mum opened the door and hugged us on the way in.

"You took your time," Mum said jokingly.

"Yeah," Aliyah responded. She was giving Mum a kiss on the cheek. "We went to suss another place out."

"And?" Mum asked.

"I'm pretty sure that's where we will get married."

Aliyah didn't pause or hesitate when she said that. I could tell that Stellar Hill was it.

"So when?" Mum asked.

Aliyah and I looked at each other. Aliyah shrugged. "As soon as we can," I said "January?" I continued with a questioning look on my face.

Mums eyes lit up. "You mean January as in like four months away?"

"Yeah, what do you think?" I asked Aliyah.

"It'll be stressful, but I'm certainly not waiting for sixteen months to get married."

"Maybe we should call tomorrow and check the availabilities and go from there?" I said.

We all walked down the hallway into the kitchen where Dad was making himself and Mum some dinner. We said our hellos and took our seats around the island bench.

"What was all the commotion about?" he asked.

"We think we found the place where we're getting married."

Aliyah had barely let Dad finish his sentence. The more she thought about it the more excited she became.

"Where is that, may I ask?"

We told Dad the details. Aliyah immediately grabbed the laptop as soon as Dad finished telling her to google the upcoming lunar calendar. Both the new moon and full moon fell on a Thursday, Dad's recommendations, as it was always a clear night. We had to decide on April the first.

"I'll call tomorrow," I said. "Hopefully that day is still available."

Aliyah's smile seemed to grow with every passing moment. I could tell it was all starting to become very real.

As we lay in bed that night watching a movie, Aliyah's head was nestled on my chest while her hand was playing with my hand. She lifted her head and turned to face me.

"What's with the smile?" I asked.

"Nothing." Her smile came with a little giggle afterward.

I took a deep breath and sighed. "I have to guess, don't I?"

Aliyah nodded, that giggle only becoming all the cheekier.

"Well, let's see." I paused for a moment to generate some ideas. "You want chocolate?"

"Well, yeah, but that's not it. Keep trying."

"Umm, you're excited to finish personal assistance traineeship in a few months and be qualified?"

A blank look shot across Aliyah's face. "Of course, but that's not it, either. Try again."

"Christmas?" I asked excitedly.

"How about I just tell you?" she muttered.

Although I wasn't facing her, I could feel the glare she was shooting at me. "That would be nice," I replied to tease her.

"I'm really excited to get married."

"That's like six months away."

"Yeah, but think of all the fun stuff we get to do now. Like wedding dress shopping and cake testing. It's just so exciting. I just can't believe I have to wait till April."

Aliyah finally took a breath. Her smile had managed to grow even larger. You couldn't wipe it off her face if you tried.

"You know we may not be able to get married until the year after?" I hesitated to say. "There has to be a date available."

"But . . . but . . .I don't want to wait that long to have our special day. I'm way too excited."

"You might have to. Your birthday is next week. There's something to be excited about."

Aliyah thumped my chest hard with her hand clenched in a fist. Four times, to be exact. Her face lit up more excitedly than I had seen for ages. She was always the type of person who enjoyed her birthday. She enjoyed every part of it.

"It's my birthday week. What did you get me?"

"As if I would tell you."

Aliyah rested her head on my chest and groaned. "Breeeennndddaaaannnnnn. You know I hate surprises."

"Too bad, you'll have to wait another week."

Aliyah pulled her phone out.

"What are you doing?"

"I should have some drinks here next weekend. I'm texting the girls."

The next week disappeared quickly, spent cleaning and preparing for her casual birthday.

Seven in the evening, her friends began to arrive. It was going to be interesting as it was the first function without Jeff accompanying Maddy, and it meant I was the only guy there. I was okay with that, as I got along well with all her friends. It was just that Jeff and I always had a great night regardless of the circumstances. We all sat around the fire pit. The hot topic was our wedding.

One by one everyone left, leaving Aliyah, Katie, Maddy, and I. It was roughly eleven o'clock, and you can imagine what Aliyah and her closest friends were up to. Wedding planning and nothing else. I cleaned up before retiring to bed, as I knew they would talk for hours, and they did just that. It was nice to see her with her closest friends, very comfortable, happy, and excited.

I was in the middle of a dream when I felt a light tap on my face. I rolled over and tried my best to get comfortable before Aliyah jumped on me and shook me with all her power.

"Oi wake up. It's Christmas," she said in a tone that could never conceal her excitement.

"It's not even light out. Are you serious? What's the time?"

You could hear the drowsiness in my non-coherent sentences like anyone who had just been woken up unexpectedly.

"I think it's like five o'clock. Come on. We have so many presents to open."

"The rule is literally no one is allowed up before seven, to give everyone time to sleep."

I didn't hear much else from her for a good minute before she got up and left the room. I sat up and wiped my eyes and slowly tried to come around. I saw a red balloon enter the room and start wondering around. I couldn't see what it was, as the end of the bed was blocking my view. Aliyah came in after it and picked it up. I jumped out of my skin for joy over what came into view.

"No freaking way. You got me a German Shepherd?"

She nodded ever so slightly with a cheeky grin on her face. Aliyah bought the puppy over to the bed, and we started playing around with her.

"I choose this one because she has the three dots down the center of her stomach. They're like buttons. She also has a patch on her forehead. I think it made her the cutest." She paused slightly before continuing. "What are you going to call her?"

I gazed upon her gorgeous little face. She had the most piercing brown eyes, and I couldn't help but smile. "Adira," I paused, completely lost in the moment. "I think her name is Adira." I turned to face Aliyah and bombarded her with questions. "Where has she been? Where did she come from? Why'd you buy her for me?"

Each question came as quick as the last not giving her the opportunity to reply.

"I was going to get you a local one, but it just was not nearly half as cute." She giggled. "Last week I called a breeder in the outback, and she said she could send the dog down as another dog was going to Melbourne, and all we had to do was pick her up."

"Oh, my God. Thank you! Thank you! Thank you! She is so gorgeous. I love you so much!"

I couldn't thank Aliyah enough. She knew how much I wanted a dog and how much I wanted a running partner. I leant over and gave her a kiss on the forehead before becoming very silent.

Aliyah noticed quickly. "What's wrong?" she asked me.

"There's nothing in the world I can get you that will match her. That's the best present ever. My present is no way near as good." I leaned over the side of the bed and grabbed a wrapped parcel.

"Stop," Aliyah said as she grabbed my arm, her other hand scratching Adira on the belly. "Adira is a thank you for the most special night of my life. I appreciate it."

"It was our special night," I said, holding Aliyah's hand, "but thank you."

CHAPTER FOURTEEN: UNTARNISHED MEMORIES

That day was the day, although I didn't feel much different. I slept alone last night at my parents, although I probably need to read up on the definition of alone. Adira, the big girl that she was becoming, spread herself over most of the bed. I sat up and wiped my eyes. Adira lifted her face to see what was happening.

"Hey, beautiful girl. How'd you sleep? You look pretty comfy!" She didn't say much, probably about as much as you expected. She just licked my face and kept staring at me. "Ready for a walk?"

Her ears pricked up as she leaped off the bed and waited by the door. I put on some shorts and runners. The day was already blissful, I could tell from the little bit of sun that I could see in the gaps in the blinds. I opened to door for her to bolt off downstairs. She probably smelled exactly what I did.

I walked past three empty beds in the upstairs living room and down the staircase to greet Mum and my groomsmen in the kitchen. As I walked into the kitchen and dining area, I was greeted by a round of hugs from my five groomsmen, while Adira did every trick in the book to get some bacon off Mum.

"How are you feeling?" Dad asked as I hugged him.

"Pretty good," I replied, nodding.

Mum interrupted us to give me a hug. "Are you sure?

Not nervous at all?"

"Honestly, not one bit. Today I get to marry my best friend."

Mum and Dad smiled. I tried to ignore it. Everyone kept talking about the wedding, wondering if I was nervous or if we prepared or planned enough. Honestly, with all the planning and preparation that had happened the last few months, I was just excited to celebrate our love. I wanted to disappear for a little bit, too.

I walked over to the kitchen. "You ready girl?" I asked Adira.

We disappeared for a few hours. The wedding wasn't until five o'clock at night, to get the perfect sunset as the ceremony happened. The day involved a hike with the dog, then some golf with the groomsmen and Aliyah's Dad. It didn't take long before it was time to start getting ready. I had a shower and put my suit on. Dad came to give me a hand with the final touches.

"You sure you're not nervous?" he asked.

"What would I be nervous about?" I responded with a grin on my face.

"Don't worry about it." Dad brushed off the smart-ass response. "Gee, you're a handsome man." He adjusted my tuxedo collar. "You look strikingly similar to me at your age."

I laughed it off. "Yeah, righto, Dad."

I stood up tall and proud next to my groomsmen and waited for the music to start playing, waited for everyone to stop talking and take their seats. The sun was setting in the background, and the moment could not have been more perfect, the bride arriving only thirty minutes late. When she got there, it was silence. I couldn't believe my eyes when I saw her. A white lace dress and a veil, as long as they come.

She looked elegant, like a princess.

A tear slid down my cheek as she walked toward me. I couldn't hide my smile, nor could she. Aliyah kept trying not to make eye contact. She kept looking toward the ground both out of shyness and to not lose her footing in her big heels. When she got to the altar, I shook her Dad's hand and took hers.

"You look amazing," I whispered.

"Love the tux," she responded.

"How was the walk? Didn't trip over?"

"The ground is so uneven."

That moment where we said our vows, word for word, Aliyah's voice still rings in my ears.

"As I take this ring, for a love so pure, through time and space, our love will endure. You are my special someone, my only wish, the person I can't wait to grow old with."

It was a strange thing to invite guests to the wedding. I wanted to declare my love for her in front of those we loved, but in that exact moment nothing else mattered. I didn't notice the sunset or smell the fields of grass. I couldn't smell dinner being made in the kitchen, and I didn't notice one other person because no one else mattered. No one else existed.

That memory will never be tainted. What she said, how she smiled. The rest of the night was strikingly like the party. Every time I was caught in a conversation or every time we had to do a task, all I can remember is glancing across the room and seeing her smile.

At nine in the evening, with the last of the sunlight peering over the horizon, it was time for our first dance together as a married couple. We elected for a slow but more upbeat song. Joined at the hip, swaying slowly. The memory of Aliyah smiling and singing to me will never fade.

We put off our honeymoon. With the wedding happening

so suddenly, money was a slight issue. That certainly wasn't about to change when I came home one day. I walked in the front door as Aliyah ran and jumped on me, immediately wrapping her legs around my waist and her arms around my neck. She gave me a kiss on the lips, a long drawn out one.

"What's up with you?" I asked.

"Can't I be excited to see my man?"

"You can, Mrs. Thomas. However, you're apparently always excited and never greet me at the door."

"This time was a bit different. I just missed you so much."

I waddled into the bedroom to put my coat down. It's kind of hard to move when somebody is wrapped around your waist constricting your movement.

I was in the middle of unbuttoning my shirt. Aliyah was sitting comfortably on the bed.

"You know how I've been a bit sick lately?" she asked.

"Yeah. How are you feeling today? Any better?" I asked. I hadn't looked up yet.

Aliyah didn't respond. She kept to silence, waiting for me to focus my attention on her. After a moment's silence, I looked up, confused.

Aliyah looked me dead in the eyes. "You're going to be a dad."

A million thoughts raced through my mind. Was she joking because she was sick? She didn't really sell it to me. She kept a dead serious face. Was that because she was worried how I'd take it? Or was that because she wanted to play a joke on me?

"Is that so?" I asked.

I went back to getting changed, trying to call her bluff.

"Brendan! I'm being serious!" she sternly added.

I looked at her again. "No jokes?"

"No jokes, I'm serious."

The smile on my face was contagious. Aliyah's face was overwhelmed with a smile, too. I leapt over straight onto the bed. "I'm going to be a dad?" I asked.

Aliyah nodded.

I'd wanted to wait till we were older, to wait until we were mature enough and financially stable, ready to have a kid. None of that crossed my mind in that moment. I wasn't stressed, nor was I nervous. I knew the future with her, everything was going to be okay.

I wrapped Aliyah up in my arms, and I couldn't stop smiling.

"That's a relief. I was worried you wouldn't take it so well." Aliyah said.

"Yeah, I'm a tad surprised that I'm this happy. It puts a dent in our plans, but I couldn't be more excited to start a family with you.

The nine months passed extraordinarily quickly. It always consisted of working, talking to the baby, and setting up the nursery. I received a call one day from Aliyah at work.

"Brendan, you need to come pick me up."

"Why?" I asked.

"I'm going into labor. It's happening so fast. You need to hurry."

I drove home immediately. She was a few weeks early but never to worry. I just wish I'd been there from the beginning. I arrived home to find Aliyah trying to sit on the couch. She was leaning forward, taking short and sharp, yet deep breaths.

I immediately raced over to her, place one hand on her back and gripped her hand with my other. She clenched my hand tight for quite some time.

"Breathe," I insisted. "Breathe."

It became time to take Aliyah to the hospital. The baby

was coming, and it wasn't stopping anytime soon. I grabbed her birth kit and her birth plan and headed straight for the car. We made our way slowly down the driveway and drove into the hospital. I called Dad on the drive the let him know to meet us at the hospital. I parked in the closest disabled spot. I figured Dad could move the car for me later. It wasn't stopping me parking there then. We headed up the ramp and into the hospital.

The nurse on duty didn't even ask for our reason. She called the other nurses and for a doctor immediately to prepare her for the birthing. We were in the delivery room when Aliyah started to look a bit pale. A nurse noticed it quickly as she was beginning to wipe the sweat off Aliyah's forehead. All the nurses and doctors immediately gave each other a look. I could feel Aliyah's grip on my hand softening. Her eyes started to roll to the back of her head.

My heart skipped a beat. I began to uncontrollably shake. All the buzzers and noises from the machines started to go crazy.

"Prepare for surgery!" the doctor demanded, pressing a button on the wall.

"What-what's going on?" I asked.

"Get him out of here!" the doctor ordered. All the nurses looked at each other before looking back at the doctor. "Quickly!"

A nurse grabbed my arm and led me from the room. I was as frozen as they come. They wheeled Aliyah out of the room and down the hall. I followed with the nurse, stride for stride.

"What's going on?" I asked.

No one answered.

"What's going on?!" I shouted. I could barely see. I had tears streaming down my face.

The doctor stopped in his tracks. The nurses continued to

wheel Aliyah into the room.

"We don't too much time to explain. Your wife has gone into cardiac arrest. We have to remove the baby immediately if either one of them are to survive."

I had become even more frozen than before. I had to lean against the wall and slowly collapsed to a seated position. The nurse sat there holding my hand. I didn't say a word. I didn't move. I was stunned.

A lot of commotion came from the room behind me, muffled, so I couldn't make out what was happening. The door opened slowly when the surgeon walked out. He crouched down in front of me. I could see the look in his eyes. I put my hand to my forehead, shaking my head. I never really heard what he said. He just placed his hand on my shoulder, bowed his head, and shook it before standing up and walking off.

I sat there frozen in time. Commotion went on around me, but all I heard was my heart pounding against my rib cage. *Thump ... thump ... thump ... thump.* The nurse who sat with me walked out of the room and then back in. She grabbed me by my hands and helped me to my feet. I walked into the room with my head bowed down. I didn't want to look up, but I had to. I put my hands to my forehead, slid them around my cheeks before covering my mouth and nose. I didn't take another step.

Aliyah was lying there, front and center with the light on her, in the middle of the table. She was pale, limp. She was lifeless. Nothing can prepare you for a moment like that. I walked closer to her, to see her face. Every part of me wished it was some cruel joke, like the one I thought she was playing on me when she told me she was pregnant. I could barely see for the tears pouring down my cheeks. I couldn't control them. I looked over at the nurses.

"The baby?" I asked. They both bowed their heads and

shook them, too. I bit both my lips at the same time before asking, "Can I have a minute?"

They both nodded and left the room. I took Aliyah's hand, icy cold, motionless, and blue. I clasped it to my chest with both my hands and burst into uncontrollable sobbing. "Why?" I cried to her.

I couldn't comprehend the situation. I couldn't stop sobbing or shaking my head, holding her hand closer to my heart than ever before.

"Thank you," I whispered. I took a moment to try to gather myself. I looked straight at her face. I still had one arm clutching hers to my chest. The other stroked her cheek, ever so gently. "Thank you, for everything. I am eternally grateful for everything you are and everything we are. I'll see you again one day, I promise."

I walked out of the room, to see the nurses holding my dead baby. "Would you like to hold her?" they asked. I shook my head. "It helps with the healing process after such a loss if you name her," one of the nurses said.

I walked straight past them into the waiting room, lifeless, like a zombie. I walked out to see mine and Aliyah's families. They were happy to see me until they sensed the mood. Mum hugged me straight away.

Everyone was standing behind her, looking at me. I shook my head. There was a unanimous reaction. Hands on mouths, a few gasps. They all held each other as Mum held me. Susan put her hand on my shoulder.

"How's Aliyah?" she asked.

The tears crept back into my eyes, I looked downwards and shook my head. Silence infected the room. "Can you guys go down there for me? I have to go," I said, parting Mum's embrace and leaving the hospital.

It was a miserable day, and I hadn't left bed for well over

a week when I heard a car pull up in the driveway. Mum opened the door. I had given her a key long back. She sat down on the bed beside me, stroked my forehead, and played with my hair.

"You ready to get moving?" she asked, her voice soft and so quiet.

I could hear the hesitation in her words. I just laid there. I acknowledged her, but I wasn't ready.

"Come on, Brendan. It's time. What are you wearing?" Mum stood up from the bed and walked over to my cupboard. She grabbed my black suit and put it on the bed next to me. "We have to go, Brendan. You'll regret not saying goodbye."

I still didn't move. By that time, Dad had come in to join her in our room. He walked over to the other side of me and put his hand on my shoulder.

"Hey, buddy."

He didn't say anything else. I don't think he knew what to say. What do you say in moments like those?

I slowly sat up and walked over to the cupboard, grabbed my black hoodie and my black tracksuit pants. I put them on, and we left. We arrived at the church where the funeral was taking place. Everyone wanted to shake my hand, but I never said a word. I wanted to thank everyone, but I hadn't spoken in over a week. I was a shell of a man.

Funerals can be a joke at times. Do we hold funerals to remember the dead? Or do we hold funerals to feel good about ourselves? Approximately four hundred people were gathered in that church, talking about their favorite memories and God's plan for us all. It was first the priest at the altar followed by her parents, her brothers, and finished with her best friends. I sat in the front row the whole time. I never moved, nor did I speak, tears uncontrollably streaming down my cheeks. Everyone was talking about their favorite memories and how they're going to miss her, but truth be told, their lives would go on. Mine? Every waking moment, I'll miss her, her smile, her infectious personality, even her smell. Even when I sleep, I can't escape it. Even though I got to enjoy being with her in my dreams, I faced a tough reality upon opening my eyes.

CHAPTER FIFTEEN: HAPPILY NEVER AFTER

The biggest slap in the face came from her mother, Susan. We were sitting around the kitchen bench drinking tea when she asked me, "How are you feeling today, Brendan?"

"No better than yesterday," I replied.

"You know it's been almost two years now. You don't have to live like this."

"We play the hand with what the gods give us."

"Did you ever think that maybe the hand the gods gave you wasn't what you were expecting?"

"What do you I mean?"

"Maybe you were supposed to find Aliyah and learn from her, but when the time came, it was for you to pass that strong bond onto someone else who needs it more."

"Are you saying I should start dating other people?"

"I just want you to be happy. Aliyah would want you to be happy."

On that weekend, it had been three and a half years since we were engaged. Every first day of the month, I would always do something small, like go out for dinner or buy her flowers. It was something small, but I never wanted the memory of our day to fade. That time, I just needed to get away. I packed my belongings and hit the road. I was on my way down to where we got engaged, although previously I hadn't been able to go near the place. I felt like I needed a weekend alone with her. The car ride was long, and I listened to the same music as the first time we drove down there together, constantly looking at the passenger seat and smiling while choking back tears. The smile was one of pain and misery, but I intended to act the whole weekend as if I was finally happy, as if Aliyah had never left. I arrived and was taken away immediately by the views, the very same way I was the first two times. I smiled and dropped my suitcase before opening a beer and sitting on the balcony. It still had that same glorious view of the top of the forest, and to the distance you could see the ocean, blissful, peaceful, beautiful. If ever I felt like Aliyah was still beside me, it was at that exact moment. The serenity was like something I had never felt before. I closed my eyes, and a smile from ear to ear crept across my face. It felt good to be home.

The whole night was one of nostalgia. Imagining that Aliyah was still there felt like Heaven.

After relaxing for a little bit, I grabbed fish-n-chips from the same shop and headed back to the place. I pretended like it was just us. It must have looked crazy, but it was nice to finally be there with just the two of us. No one else in the world ever mattered, and no one ever will. I lit some candles and put on our songs. I laid on the balcony and listened.

I had the biggest smile on my face while I was laying there, looking at the stars. It was the first time I had smiled in years and meant it. I remembered when I was in the hospital and first found out I had lost her. It was the same as the day of her funeral. After many hours of remembering how sad I had been, remembering the crying and rage fits, I blew out the candles. It was time to get some rest.

That night ended like every other night, me camped out under the stars talking to Aliyah. Asking her about her day and telling her about mine. Questioning what the afterlife is like. Although this time, I wasn't sad. I gave my favorite photo of us two a kiss, smiled, and before falling asleep, whispered, "I'll see you soon, beautiful, I promise."

So, you tell me how I'm supposed to be happy, friend, because I'm lost. If I was supposed to be happy, she would still be here. They would still be here. I had my happiness, and I'll forever be grateful, but there is no happy future for me. There is no smile. There are no laughs, just nothing. At the start, everyone understands, the reason you're upset, the reason you're angry, the reason you're lethargic and don't want to talk, the reason you can't see a bright future for yourself. Time passes. People start asking *why is he angry? Why is he upset? He needs to put it behind him and move on.*

None of that fazed me because it's expected that time will heal your wounds. I knew many people would never experience the bond Aliyah and I shared. That's why they could never possibly understand. We loved more in those few years than many will ever experience in a whole lifetime, and we still do now. If there is an afterlife, I know she's thinking of me. I also know they will both forever live on in my heart. That's what true love is.

On that perfect night, we'd promised each other an eternity. Some people say I'll love you forever, but there is a physical bond. I still love Aliyah, and Aliyah still loves me. I feel her every time I talk to her, and I feel her every time I think of our memories. Then I get upset. Over time, the memory of her smile fades, and her laugh no longer echoes in my ears. The pillows and her clothes that I never washed lose her smell and begin to smell like me. Tell my how I'm supposed to be happy because I'm not ready for a life without her.

The next day started very differently to others. I woke up and got on with my duties, rather than lying in bed for hours on end, miserable. Although I had paid for two nights, I packed my bags and headed home. It was a Saturday. Over three years since our perfect night, and I couldn't bear to be in the same spot that night. It was already going to be rough. My drive home was complete silence. A couple hours of no noise other than the car engine which got drowned out over time. I was lost for words. I smiled and kissed the photo I carried around with me at all times.

It was three in the afternoon and my family was at the local football. They always went to watch my brother play. I headed home and lay on my bed. I couldn't get Aliyah out of my head, I knew it was time. I walked outside to spend my final moments with Adira. She licked my face. I thanked her for everything she had done. I know she was a dog, but I think she knew it was our last embrace. I turned on the bath on and began to write,

Dear Family,

To Dad, Mum, Ben, and Theresea. Please understand. Words can't truly describe how much I appreciate you. We shared some rough moments during the years, but you helped shape me into who I became. You cared for me and loved me. I'm sorry I haven't been that happy son or brother the past few years. Please forgive me and take care of Adira. Please take care of yourselves and appreciate every moment. Appreciate growing old as there are some of us who aren't lucky enough to do so. Please understand that for every bad memory we shared, we also shared one hundred good ones, so don't regret anything and be at peace. To Trevor and Susan, I'm sorry I didn't protect your daughter like I promised. You guys took me into your home and loved me, and I'll be forever grateful. I promise I'll find her now and take the best care of her. I want you all to know that I'm not doing this for apologies or for sympathy. It's just impossible to move on. When Aliyah looked into my eyes and smiled, knowing I was the reason why was the best feeling in the world, one that can never be replaced. I'd go through everything again just to see her smile at me one last time, to hold her in my arms. After everything that happened, to be loved and appreciated by her and the way she made me feel, it's the rea-

son why I will forever remain privileged.

The page was stained with tear drops as I left it on the bathroom bench. I climbed into the bath and grabbed the knife. I took the knife to my wrists. It was time. I smiled and relaxed back against the porcelain. I took my wedding ring off and clasped it in my hands along with Aliyah's. I kissed them and smiled. I cradled the rings in my chest and closed my eyes. I threw my head back and smiled as I whispered to myself.

"As I take this ring, for a love so pure.
Through time and space, our love will endure.
You are my special someone, my only wish,
The person I can't wait to grow old with."

You may also enjoy the following from eXtasy Books Inc:

A Time to Dance
Jojo Brown

Excerpt

From where she stood on the balcony of her seventh-story apartment, she knew that with the slightest glance he would be able to see right through the thin cotton blouse she had on. That was the whole idea though, wasn't it?

She wanted him to look, wanted him to see her, wanted to distract him — even if just for a moment. After all, he had distracted her for well over a week now and Celeste figured it was time for a little pay back.

At thirty-two years of age, Celeste had come to the point in her life where she was very happy and content with the way most of it was going. The ability to write was her passion for as long as she could remember. Her mother would tell you — if she were in one of her seldom kind moods — Celeste had been born with a pencil in her hand and a vivid imagination.

Straight out of college she got a good job at the international trades firm owned by a friend of her father. Everyone felt, except Celeste, that with her natural flare with words, she should be happy and content with her position.

To the horror of her parents, she had walked away from it four years ago. Since then, she'd happily written romances and she truly felt that it was the perfect job for her. It was much better than a stuffy office with proposals and reports for things she didn't really care about to write.

Now she made her living softly wrapped in the whites and creams of her airy apartment. She was her own time manager, deadline keeper and more importantly — her own supervisor. Of course, her editor gave her the main deadlines, but within that time frame Celeste was in control of everything.

She loved her job, her apartment and, until recently, her neighbourhood. When they first saw the renovated office building in the city's core, her family was obscenely concerned. To begin with, they didn't like the idea of her living alone in the city.

Even on the day that she moved in, her mother tried to convince her to go back to her office job and live in the cramped box with tight security, within easy reach of her constant advice.

Oh yes — her mother had always been a vault of good advice. Everything from what kind of schools to attend to whom she should date, had come under the heading of mother knows best, until the day Celeste moved into the city.

Mother simply could not understand why Celeste felt the need to escape the corporate world, nor could she see the sense in moving away from her own class.

The family's class was so ridiculously over and above most of the people she dealt with, it was as if they were from a different universe. She came from old money, born with the proverbial silver spoon balanced between her pink lips. She'd grown up in a vast house filled with butlers, chauffeurs, maids and nannies and had always bristled against the expectations of her parents.

They felt she needed to marry well. In other words, a man handpicked by them. Then they expected her to keep a good home, lord herself over her own army of servants. The only work expected of her would be to help with whatever good cause run by the Ladies Auxiliary of the Country Club at the time.

Celeste couldn't stand it anymore. She needed to spread her wings, become her own person and desperately needed to put some mileage, between her and her overbearing parents. They had not forgiven her yet, perhaps they never would.

Her apartment had been just the ticket with its large windows, open floor plan and fantastic view. She quickly settled into the life she'd always dreamed of. Her favourite place was out on the balcony. From there, she looked over the top of any building around and marvelled in the beauty of the lazy, dark river running through the centre of the city. At least it was, until very recently.

When the construction started in the empty lot next to Celeste's building, she was sorely unimpressed. The noise alone was enough to drive any sane person to the nut house. Then of course, as the heavy machines rumbled in and out all day, the quietly eclectic neighbourhood had lost most of its appeal.

Until this, she had always relished her time at the computer beside an open window. The fresh breeze on a spring day or the sound of light summer rain always helped take her mind away from the city, from the sometimes-harsh reality of life. For a writer, the ability to escape the confines of reality is almost as important as air.

She kept the window shut tight, since to have it open even the smallest crack would be to invite a torrent of dust and unpleasant odours into her sanctuary.

The assault carried on for more weeks than she cared to remember. She tried sleeping through the day in order to write in the quiet hours of the night. Forget that. To get any proper rest when the very building shuddered from the force exerted so near its foundations was impossible.

She tried to take her laptop and head out each morning to a park or a coffee shop. Then spend the day tucked away in a back booth, sipped coffees and nibbled on whichever pastry struck her fancy while her fingers tapped furiously away at the keyboard.

The few customers that drifted in and out, acted as a wonderfully calming background noise for her efforts. It was sort of fun. No one noticed her as she sat quietly and watched the ordinary lives of everyday people. It all worked superbly—for a while. Then the schools let out for summer break and it became impossible to find a spot in the city without noisy distractions.

After one final attempt to find solitude within the urban jungle, Celeste solemnly slunk back to her not so quiet corner of the world. Her idea to hide in the shade of an ancient maple tree in the back corner of a local park had gone the way of the dinosaurs. Six rather rambunctious, loud teen-aged boys armed with a Frisbee had laid claim to that corner of the park.

To her amazement, the ugly iron monster had grown to great heights without her notice. It stood majestically above the plywood walls, which surrounded its base. As she approached this unwelcome intruder in her world, catcalls and obscenities assaulted Celeste's ears.

The men who scurried around upon the skeleton of the creature they helped bring to life gave it a voice. Not only was it ugly and messy, it was rude and obnoxious.

After that day, just going out to the shops became a chore, one she put off as much as she could.

Celeste began to pray for rain as this would keep the animals at bay. The site would be blessedly quiet, other than the patter of raindrops. She could work and she could walk past the site undisturbed and some of the smell would wash away with the dust.

Yes, rainy days were heaven for Celeste.

Somehow, over the months, the intrusion stopped bothering her quite so much and she got more work done. Whether the noise lessened or she simply grew accustomed to it all is hard to say.

Nevertheless, it happened.

Celeste returned to her usual routine. Up with the sun, she had her morning coffee and bagel on the balcony and then headed inside for a shower and hours at the computer.

Arlene, her editor, was very pleased with this return to normal. Her fear had been that Celeste's work would suffer a permanent lapse.

Many frantic phone calls came in from Arlene about the latest manuscript. Celeste had tried every kind of manoeuvring tactic she could think of to appease her. However, Arlene continued to suffer from slight anxiety attacks.

Once talented fingers started flying over the keyboard again, Arlene had relaxed.

One morning in mid-July, she stood in the foyer of her building with one of her neighbours, Alice. Celeste had just returned from a quick trip to the bakery for fresh rolls and, once again, the rude comments from above got under her skin. She started to complain about the construction and the low-class workers on it. She truly hoped to find some sort of sympathizer in Alice.

"If those dirty, foul-mouthed Neanderthals knew how much they impacted people's lives, they would probably send a huge grunting cheer to the heavens. I can't imagine any of them giving a damn about anyone else's life outside of how uncomfortable they can make them."

Alice, her wonderfully outrageous, bohemian upstairs neighbour, who had been the first to welcome her when she moved in, simply laughed. "Oh, they're not that bad! I actually kinda like the fact that they watch my girls jiggle when I flounce past them, it feeds my ego. Besides, I get a kick outta thinking of them trying to get around up there, with massive hard-ons. Of course, in my fantasy, they are all extremely well-endowed." She held her sides as though they'd cramped from her uproarious laughter.

"Oh, Alice. That's disgusting!"

"What is?" she sobered abruptly.

"Thinking about them sexually, well endowed or not, then talking about it," Celeste huffed. "I certainly don't want to think of any of them like that."

Alice stared intently into Celeste's dark eyes and gave her two cents worth of free advice. "Girl, you need to get laid."

Astounded at her friend's bluntness, Celeste felt her face turn crimson. "What the hell is that supposed to mean?"

"Well, when's the last time you had some hot stud buried between your thighs?"

A quick, nervous glance around the small area between the front doors and the elevator assured her no one was close enough to overhear their conversation. Celeste admitted, "It has been a while. I'm too busy to even think about it."

"What's to think about?" Alice gasped. "God, if I don't get some at least three times a week I start looking at bananas and cucumbers down at the market in a whole new light. Seriously, how long has it been?"

"Well, Mike and I split up six months ago and we hadn't done anything for at least a month before the split. So I guess that makes it seven months."

"Holy shit! How do you survive that long without it? No wonder you have all this pent-up anxiety. Seriously, your insides must be damn near ready to explode from the need for release. You definitely need to have a screaming orgasm and soon, then you'll see the world in a whole new light."

The two of them stepped into the elevator. Celeste kept her eyes on the mail in her hands as though someone had sent her the big prize from the lottery and she had to figure out which envelope held the fortune.

"It is not that bad, Alice," she mumbled.

"Well, hon, once you're ready to admit that you still have a libido, give me a call. I have all kinds of friends that would be more than willing to help you chill out."

"I have seen some of those friends of yours," Celeste laughed. She pictured the unsavoury sorts she'd seen come and go from Alice's apartment. "No thanks."

"You could always just come up sometime, when I'm home alone. I am real good at relieving stress," Alice said as the doors opened on Celeste's floor. "I guarantee you would feel a hell of a lot better after."

Celeste held the door open and turned back to Alice, "While that is a very kind offer, Alice, I've always been an outy-gal. I like the feel, taste and smell of a man, the way his sexuality is right out there for all to see. It's great to see the effect I have on him with just a glance."

Alice stepped very close to Celeste and stroked her cheek affectionately. "You'll never know what you're missing in life if you don't try new things, sweetheart."

With the briefest of kisses on her cheek, Alice slipped past Celeste and skipped down the hall. "I'm gonna take the stairs," she called as she pulled the elastic from her flaming red hair. The long unruly curls fanned out behind her.

ABOUT THE AUTHOR

Australian Mathew Di-Giusto is a first-time author with a passion for romance. Intrigued with writing from a young age, Mathew spent the majority of his adolescent years reading young adult novels and writing short stories. Currently a student at Swinburne University, he lives in Victoria with his wife, Milly, and two Siberian huskies.